TIME STON

MW00941262

TREACHERY

IN THE ANCIENT

LABORATORY

Written by
Karla Warkentin

Illustrated by
Ron Adair

COLLECT THEM ALL!
Rescue in the Mayan Jungle
Mystery in the Medieval Castle
Treachery in the Ancient Laboratory
Terror in Hawk's Village

Equipping Kids for Life

Faith Building Guide
Ages 9 and up
Reverence

An Imprint of Cook Communications Ministries
Colorado Springs, CO

A Faith Building Guide can be
found on page 139.

Faith Kidz® is an imprint of Cook Communications Ministries
Colorado Springs, Colorado 80918
Cook Communications, Paris, Ontario
Kingsway Communications, Eastbourne, England

TREACHERY IN THE ANCIENT LABORATORY
©2004 by Karla Marie Krahn-Warkentin

First printing, 2004
Printed in the United States of America.
1 2 3 4 5 6 7 8 9 10 Printing/Year 08 07 06 05 04

Editor: Heather Gemmen
Design Manager: Nancy L. Haskins
Cover Designer: Image Studios
Cover Illustrator: Ron Adair
Interior Designer: Pat Miller

To Mom, for showing me how to love,
and to Dad, for teaching me how to dream.

Thank you to:

My beloved husband, Randy, for your
unwavering support and endless patience.
I couldn't do this without you.

Elaine Wright Colvin, for your ongoing mentoring and encouragement.
Your words of wisdom make the journey smoother.

Carol Ann Hiemstra, for your excellent suggestions,
additions, and fine-tuning.

Ron Adair, for the beautiful covers.
Your creativity and skill astound me.

Dr. Gus Konkel, for helping me understand the
third commandment in a deeper, broader way.

My Westside prayer team: Wayne and Phyllis Banman, Rachel Dyck,
Ingrid Friesen, Linda Janzen, Cindy Klassen, Marie Peters,
Mary Poetker, Sharon Toews, and Grace Warkentin—
I cherish each one of you.

And finally, to the entire Cook Communications Ministries team,
especially my editor, Heather Gemmen. Your dedication, skill,
and patience have been a blessing.

K.W.

"You shall not misuse the name
of the LORD your God,
for the LORD will not hold anyone guiltless
who misuses his name."

Exodus 20:7

Contents

ONE

THE STONE

CRITICAL:
ﬆﬆ

Come on, you can do it. Please turn on, please, please, please," begged Josh. He was sitting on his bedroom floor in his pajamas: boxer shorts, one of his dad's old T-shirts, and a backwards baseball cap that covered his blond hair. His sister, Ellen, sat cross-legged on his left, and his twin brother, Will, sat on his right. Josh clutched the stone even tighter in his hand and wiggled back and forth, trying to get his backpack into a comfortable position. "This stupid bag is already driving me crazy. I wonder how long I'll have to carry it."

"If it's so uncomfortable, maybe you shouldn't bring it. What did you pack?" asked Ellen. She sat there, poised, her back completely straight. Many years of ballet classes had given her perfect posture. Josh never had been able to understand why anyone would want to dance around in slippers and a frilly tutu, but a lot of things about girls didn't make sense to him.

"I need every single thing in this bag. Look, I'll show you." Josh unzipped his backpack and pulled out six dirty, rolled-up socks, none of which matched the others; a slingshot; his Bible; a broken flashlight; $1.37 in loose change; Rasputin, his favorite teddy bear; a wrinkly old jacket; a half-empty bag of red licorice; and a handful of elastic bands. "I think that's all." He thrust his hand in even deeper and rummaged around the bottom some more. "Oh, I guess not," he added, grinning, as he triumphantly pulled out two pairs of clean underwear. "The only reason I packed these is because I knew it would make Mom happy. I probably won't need them."

"That's for sure. You never change your underwear," agreed Will.

Ellen shook her head. "I don't know how anyone could wear the same pair for two weeks in a row. That's disgusting."

"Sometimes I wear the same pair for a month."

"And you're proud of it?"

Josh shrugged his shoulders. "What did you pack?"

"A bunch of clothes, six headbands, a bandana, three flavors of lip gloss, my Bible, and a blanket and pillow. I'm ready for anything."

"But half of that is girl stuff."

"So?" At fourteen, three years older than her brothers, Ellen knew better than to let Josh's comments bug her. She grabbed one of his elastic bands and tied her brown hair into a ponytail.

"What do you think you're doing?"

"Making a ponytail." The condescending tone in her voice was unmistakable.

"But now I'll have girl germs on my stuff. Yuck!"

Will cleared his throat to get their attention. "You guys don't know a thing about packing. I've got it down pat." He was dressed in combat fatigues, and a pair of binoculars hung around his neck. He unzipped three of his vest pockets and started pulling out his supplies: a box of waterproof matches, several sizes of flashlights, mosquito netting, a compass, a spool of fishing line, and some lures. He stuck out his chest and smiled, looking completely pleased with himself. "And that's just one pocket. That's what I call being prepared. I'm ready for anything." He took his glasses off, blew on them until they were foggy, and then pulled a cloth handkerchief out of a different vest pocket and gave them a thorough cleaning.

"What's in your backpack?" asked Josh.

Will put his glasses back on, unzipped his backpack, and peered inside. "A portable camp stove, bottled water, enough dehydrated food for a week, a sleeping bag, and a calendar."

"Where'd you get all that stuff?"

"From the garage. Dad said I could borrow it if I put it back."

"No wonder your backpack's so full. Why do you need a calendar?" asked Ellen.

"So I can figure out how long we're gone."

"How are you going to carry all that? It must weigh a ton."

"We'll take turns."

"What?" exclaimed Ellen.

"When Josh's licorice runs out and you're both hungry, you'll come running. If you want to eat, you'll have to take a turn."

"That's not fair. You can't expect us carry your stuff," protested Josh.

Will furrowed his brow. "Why not? I think it's a great idea."

"I'm packing my own food. I'm not doing your work." Josh ran down the stairs to the kitchen and returned a minute later with a bag of cookies tucked under his arm. He dropped them into his backpack and jammed the rest of his stuff on top.

"Josh, be careful. You'll break the cookies," said Ellen.

"So?"

"Then all you'll have is a bunch of crumbs."

He shrugged his shoulders. "What do we do now?"

"We need to get the time stone to work. Try touching it again," suggested Ellen.

Several months ago, Josh had discovered a stone embedded in their front lawn. It was covered with strange carved symbols that no one in his family could decipher. After inspecting it with his dad, Josh left it in the garage for safekeeping. Late that night, he and his brother and sister crept into the garage. As they stood there looking at the stone, a small hole opened on one side of it and it began projecting pictures onto a nearby wall. Overcome by fear, Josh accidentally brushed against the stone as it was projecting a picture of a jungle, and he and his siblings were transported to an ancient Mayan village.

A month later, the stone started up again. This time Will slammed his hand down onto it as it projected a picture of a castle onto their bedroom wall, and they time traveled to a castle in medieval England.

On both trips, the three of them encountered a difficult problem that was plaguing the people they visited. Through the power of God, they helped the people solve their problem. The stone was the key to their adventures, and even though they were terrified at times, they were eager to go again.

"Before you do anything, there's one thing you have to remember. When the pictures come on the wall, don't touch the stone right away. We need to see all our options. The first place might not be the best one," said Will.

Josh completely ignored him. He reached over and covered the stone with his palm. Nothing happened. He picked it up and flipped it back and forth from hand to hand. Nothing happened. He tossed it into the air and caught it. Still nothing happened.

Frustrated, he handed the stone to Ellen. She gently ran her fingertips over it, trying to find the spot where the light came out, but its surface was completely smooth; she couldn't detect a break anywhere. "I don't know how it works. Maybe we can't turn it on."

"Here, let me try," said Will.

"What? You mean you actually want to go?" asked Josh.

"I think I'm ready. Now that we've had two trips, I know what to expect. I packed everything I could possibly need—"

"—And more," added Ellen.

Will shot her a dirty look. "I'm just trying to be prepared."

"Whatever you do, don't throw up, okay? It's really embarrassing when you do that," said Josh.

"But I can't help it."

"That doesn't mean we like it. It's so annoying."

"But it's not my fault."

"It is so. If you weren't such a wimp, you wouldn't throw up all the time."

"I'm not a wimp. I helped you fight that guy in the jungle, and I rode that huge horse in England, remember?"

"You finally fought the shaman after you wimped out on everything else, and you didn't really ride that horse. You just sat on it while it galloped. That's completely different than riding."

"It is not."

"Is so." Josh stood up and struck his teapot pose, with one arm suspended in the air above his head and the other bent, resting on his hip, like the little teapot in the nursery rhyme. "Hi," he said in a high-pitched voice, "my name is Will. I try to act tough, but I'm really not. I'd just shrivel up and die if my little brother didn't take care of me, because without him I'm just a pathetic weakling."

Will pulled Josh's cap down over his eyes and stomped out of the room.

Ellen uncrossed her legs and stood up. "So much for that. Why do you have to be so mean?"

"Because he annoys me. He thinks he's got everything figured out, but we both know he doesn't have a clue. Right?"

Ellen tried to stifle a smile but didn't quite succeed. "I suppose."

"Come on, Ellen, you know I'm right. Look at him. He's dressed in camouflage, although I suppose that's better than those fancy clothes he usually wears. We managed just fine on our other trips without that stuff."

"I still think you should be nicer. There's no excuse for being mean. Go apologize."

"I'll talk to him later. In the meantime, I'm taking some of these." Josh grabbed a pack of matches from Will's backpack and stuffed them into his T-shirt pocket. "You never know when they might come in handy."

A week later, Josh woke up in the middle of the night to the sight of a laboratory on his bedroom wall. A tall, thin man dressed in a long, flowing cape stood hunched over a maze of glass containers. Murky gray liquid trickled through them, falling one drop at a time into a beaker below.

Josh jumped off his top bunk and landed on the foot of Will's bed. "Wake up! The stone's on—it's working!"

Will sat up, blinking rapidly as he looked around the room. It took him a few seconds to get his bearings. Once he was fully awake, he put on his glasses. "Go get Ellen, quick," he gasped.

Josh sprinted out of the room and returned with Ellen a few seconds later. They plopped down on the bed beside Will. "I can't believe it. It's finally time. That place looks great," exclaimed Josh.

Will held up his hand. "No, wait! We need to see all our options. There might be a better one."

The picture on the wall started to fade.

Josh turned to Ellen. "Do you want to go?"

"No, wait!" interrupted Will. He grabbed Josh's arm.

"Let go of me! I want to go!" shrieked Josh.

"No, wait!"

Josh reached across Will with his other arm and slammed his hand down on the time stone. A large whoosh of sound filled the air. Josh was pushed back onto Will's bed, and a dark whirlwind picked them up and carried them away.

TWO

GOLDEN LANE

J osh opened his eyes. The ground beneath him was hard, the air was cool, and the stars were just beginning to fade as the sky brightened. He sat up, shivering, and pulled his arms against his chest. "Guys, get up! Look at the little houses!"

Ellen slowly sat up behind him. Will lay there groaning. "I don't feel good. Give me the time stone. I want to go home." Suddenly he leaned over and grabbed his stomach. "Oh, no," he mumbled, before promptly throwing up.

Josh stood up without acknowledging his brother's discomfort. The winding cobblestone lane where they landed was not much wider than his shoulders, and the houses that bordered it were only two heads taller than him. "Look at these houses. They look like they could be made out of Lego," he exclaimed.

The houses had been built so close together that each one touched the next. They were backed by a tall stone wall, and their pastel colors—a mottled blue, pinkish red, and pale yellow—gave the street a cheerful flair. Each house had a main door, one or two small windows, and a plume of smoke drifting out of its chimney. Many had window boxes filled with bright flowers. The entire street was scrupulously clean; there wasn't a speck of litter or dirt anywhere.

Josh's eyes grew wide as he continued to study his surroundings. "Maybe we've turned into giants, or maybe we're in a land of leprechauns."

Ellen walked over to him, weaving back and forth. She grabbed his shoulder to help keep her balance. "It's not fair. Whenever we time travel, I always feel lousy, like I was flattened by a steamroller or something, and you get up as if nothing happened."

"What can I say? You're a wimp, and I'm not. Did you know we might be giants?"

Ellen snorted. "Giants? You've got to be kidding. Here I am, looking to you for sympathy, and that's the best you can come up with?"

"Let's look around before the little people get up. We need to get our bearings."

"Where do you think we are?"

Will groaned. "It doesn't matter. We need to go home. Give me the stone," he ordered, still sprawled on the ground but trying to look like he was in charge.

"William MacKenzie, get up! We've already been through this two times before. You know we won't find the stone until our trip is over. We may as well get going," said Ellen.

"She's right. You're wasting our time," added Josh.

"I'll get up on one condition."

"What's that?" asked Ellen, sounding rather impatient.

"Josh has to promise not to touch the stone next time. I'm positive there were better places to go than this stupid little village."

"You don't know enough about this village to decide if it's stupid. Put a lid on it until we figure things out, okay?"

"Oh, oh. Ellen's mad. If I were you, I'd get up. I wouldn't mess with her," said Josh.

Will struggled to his feet and shuffled down the lane, still looking green. Josh and Ellen followed behind, single file.

Josh turned to his sister. "Where do you think we are?"

"I don't know. My first impression was that we were somewhere in Scandinavia, but I don't think that's right. It's not cold enough."

"Where's Scandinavia?"

"It's those little countries above Germany, you know, like Norway,

Finland, and Denmark, and, since I know you're wondering, the people there are normal sized."

"Oh." Josh looked disappointed.

"Don't listen to her. She has no idea what she's talking about." Will pointed to a hand-painted sign with squiggly letters above one of the doorways. "Look at the writing on the buildings. I don't know what language that is, but I'm quite sure it's not Scandinavian. It's more likely Eastern European."

"You don't know anything about Eastern Europe," said Josh.

"I do so. It consists of several countries: Czechoslovakia, Hungary, and Poland."

"And how do you know that?"

"Quit interrupting. I wasn't finished yet. To answer your question, I read a book on Eastern Europe last year, and actually, I was incorrect in listing Czechoslovakia as one of the countries. It split into two countries in 1993, the Czech Republic and Slovakia. The Slavic languages, which are based on the Latin alphabet, are spoken in that part of the world."

"Thank you, smart boy." Josh looked over to Ellen. "At least he's participating now."

"I liked it better when he was grumpy and quiet."

Will stuck out his tongue at her. He was about to continue his history lesson when he was interrupted by a sharp creak. The door of the blue house two buildings ahead was slowly opening. They ducked behind the house nearest them—it had a low wooden fence that bordered a small flower garden. Josh pressed his back against the wall and tried not to move.

A young boy about the twins' age came out of the blue house. Clumps of hair stood straight up from his head like little horns, and his left cheek was covered in red creases from his pillow. He was quite thin, similar to Will in height and build, and wore a pair of wool knickers and a loose white shirt, which was almost as pale as he was. He rubbed his eyes. Josh could hear his shoulder blades crack as he stretched.

The boy turned in their direction and was walking along absent-mindedly when he spotted them. He jumped back in surprise and mumbled something.

"Did you understand that?" whispered Josh.

"I think he asked us what we're doing," said Ellen.

Josh stood up. "Hi. My name's Josh, and this is my sister Ellen and my brother Will. We're just looking around."

Will grabbed him by the leg and pulled. "Don't say that. He'll think we don't know what we're doing," he hissed.

Josh jerked his leg away. "But we don't know. That's how this works. Sit still and be quiet while I do the talking."

Will glared at him, his cheeks blazing. "No, you sit still and be quiet. I'll do the talking. I guarantee I'll do a better job than you." He turned to the boy. "What's your name?" he snarled.

The boy looked him over from head to toe, not saying a word. Will was quite a sight in his rumpled pajamas.

"I said, 'What's your name?'" demanded Will.

The boy just stared.

Josh took a step forward. "Just ignore my brother. He's a real pain sometimes. Can you tell me where we are?"

"You're standing on the street."

Josh gave him a sheepish look. "I know that. What city are we in?"

"You're in Prague."

"Where's that?"

"In the Kingdom of Bohemia."

"Bohemia? I've never heard of that before," sputtered Josh.

"It's in Czechoslovakia, you know, Eastern Europe, the place I was telling you about before," grumbled Will. "Why won't he talk to me?"

"Probably because you're so difficult. I wouldn't talk to you either if I didn't have to. Now be quiet so I can concentrate."

Josh turned back to the boy. "What year is it?"

"1610."

Josh's jaw dropped. He and Ellen looked at each other. "That's only two hundred years after we were in England. It's going to be different here," said Ellen.

"We're in the 1600s? That means no electricity, cars, grocery stores—" said Will.

"—Or computers or Internet," added Josh.

"What are you talking about?" interrupted the boy.

"Oh, sorry. We didn't mean to ignore you. Do you live here?" asked Josh.

"I live with my uncle, Pepik."

"What's your name?"

"Benjamin, but everyone calls me Ben for short."

"How come I can't understand him?" interrupted Will.

"I don't know. Be quiet and think nice thoughts. Maybe that will help," suggested Ellen.

"What does your uncle do?" asked Josh.

"He's an alchemist for the emperor. I'm his assistant. One day I'll be an alchemist, too."

Josh gave him a confused look. "What's an alchemist?"

"Someone who's carrying out the *Great Work*, you know, making the elixir of life, the 'philosopher's stone.' That's what everyone who lives on the lane is seeking."

"Why would a philosopher be trying to make a stone? Aren't they supposed to be sitting around, trying to understand things that no one really cares about?"

Will coughed loudly. "That's not what a philosopher does."

Ben scrunched up his nose and squinted at the two of them. "A philosopher is a person who tries to figure things out, often using science."

"You obviously have a different definition of a philosopher than we do. They sound like scientists," said Ellen.

"What's an elixir?" asked Josh.

"It's a magical potion," replied Ben.

"Really? What does it do?"

Ben's eyes gleamed with delight. "The one we are trying to create has two main properties. It changes any metal it touches into gold, and if you drink it, it will make you immortal."

"You're joking, right?" said Josh.

"No," said Ben, looking slightly insulted. "Alchemy has been practiced for over a thousand years by some very important people, like Morenius, the Jewish hermit; Albertus Magnus and his student Thomas Aquinas; Nicholas Flamel, who translated *The Book of Abraham, the Jew*; and Basil Valentine, just to name a few."

Will's eyes opened wide and he smiled. "Hey, I heard that. I can understand him now."

Josh let out a low growl. "Good. Now quit interrupting." He turned to his new friend. "Can you get me some of this elixir stuff?"

"It's not that easy. For some, the Great Work takes their entire life, and they never master it. For others, it comes much easier."

"Has your uncle ever made this stuff?" asked Ellen.

"He's come close several times, but the conditions were not quite right, and in the end he didn't succeed." Ben leaned forward and lowered his voice to a whisper. "I think he's getting close again, but we'll have to see. He's not sure he has enough faith."

"Can we meet your uncle?" asked Josh.

"Of course. Come in, I'll show you around." Ben walked toward the door. "By the way, where are you from?"

"We're from Canada, a country across the ocean," said Ellen.

"Really? How did you get here?"

"You probably won't believe this, but we time traveled."

"Hmm. That's interesting. I've heard of that before."

Josh, Will, and Ellen looked at each other, surprised by his response. Before they had a chance to reply, Ben pushed open the door and led them inside his little blue house.

It took a minute for Josh's eyes to adjust to the light. The house consisted of one room—a combination laboratory, kitchen, bedroom, and study. A thick layer of soot inside the windows blocked most of the light.

To Josh's left, a wooden table sat haphazardly in the middle of the floor. It was covered with books and miscellaneous glass containers. Two rickety chairs were pulled up to one of its sides. To his right, a wooden chest with dozens of tiny drawers was pushed against the wall, each drawer meticulously labeled. A bookshelf and small cot lined the back wall.

More books, several sets of mortars and pestles, some long-handled spoons, an odd assortment of glass jars filled with dried leaves, and a variety of other laboratory equipment were piled willy-nilly throughout the room. The floor was so crowded by mounds of charcoal, a round globe on a wooden stand, and more glass laboratory equipment that it was impossible to walk in a straight line from one side of the room to the other. And if all this wasn't enough, a stuffed baby crocodile hung from the center of the ceiling.

Despite the disorder, the room was surprisingly clean. The floor had been swept, the table wiped, and the bed was neatly made. Even the wooden chest had been buffed to a shine.

Josh stood there, awestruck. "If we let our room get this messy, Mom would probably ground us for a month," he whispered.

"And she definitely wouldn't let you hang a baby crocodile from your ceiling," added Ellen.

The sound of someone sucking air followed by a loud snore caught their attention. Off to their right, near the fancy chest, an old man slept on a tattered velvet chair in front of a small portable furnace. A strange-looking glass flask, round at the bottom with a tall skinny neck, bubbled away on top of it. The old man's feet rested on a pile of wood. One of his red leather slippers had fallen off, revealing his big toe, which poked through the hole of his white stocking. The hem of his long gray robe pooled haphazardly on the floor around him, and his arms dangled over the sides of the chair, one hand holding bellows and the other a pair of tongs.

Ben rushed over to him. "Uncle Pepik, wake up."

The old man jerked upright and rubbed his eyes. "What . . . Oh . . . Did I fall asleep?"

Ben nodded.

"How could I do that at such a critical time? Shame on me. My dear boy, you must keep me awake tonight at any cost."

Ben smiled. "We'll see."

His uncle gave him a stern look. "Benjamin, I am serious. Much is at stake. You know the consequences if we do not succeed. I cannot let the fire burn down at this critical stage."

"I'm sorry, Uncle. You're right. We'll make a plan for tonight. Everything will be fine."

"And who are your friends?"

"This is Josh, Will, and Ellen. They time traveled here from across the ocean."

Ben's uncle stood up so he could examine them. He was almost completely bald, except for a border of straggly red hair that lined the base of his skull. A bushy red beard covered most of his pasty white face. He pulled the red sash around his waist tighter and absentmindedly shuffled across the room; his bowlegs repeatedly bumped into the stacks of books that littered the floor.

"Pepik Zelenka," he said, holding out his hand. "Pleased to meet you."

Josh returned the handshake. "Josh MacKenzie," he replied, "and my brother Will and sister Ellen."

Will leaned over to his brother. "Is he the man from the picture on the wall?" he whispered.

"No. The guy on the wall was skinny."

"What brings you to Prague?" asked Pepik.

"We don't know yet. We go on these time-travel journeys every once in a while. The whole thing just sort of happens. We don't have much say in it," explained Josh.

"Hmm, interesting. Are you familiar with alchemy?"

"No, sir. Your nephew told us a bit about it. I'd like some of that elixir, though."

Pepik chuckled. "So would most of Prague, or at least those who know of its existence. His Majesty Rudolph II is particularly keen to obtain some, although I'm not sure that would be good. It would only prolong his madness."

"Who's Rudolph?"

"Our emperor. He's not entirely to blame for his condition. Insanity runs in his family."

"That doesn't sound good. Poor guy," said Ellen.

"He will be poor if he keeps spending money the way he has been of late. I don't know why he needs all those gimcracks and gewgaws; I can't say they do him a bit of good."

Josh looked at his brother and sister. Ellen gave him an encouraging smile, but Will ignored him. He was too busy examining Pepik's laboratory and furnace.

Suddenly Pepik gasped. "My goodness, I've said far too much. I am grateful for the assistance of the emperor. Why, it is he who makes my work here possible." He furrowed his eyebrows. "Are you in his service?"

"I have no idea what you're talking about. We've never even met the guy," said Josh.

Pepik let out a sigh of relief. "Good. For a minute I thought you might be spies. I swear His Majesty can tell I'm getting close. There has been no peace of late, and all the interruptions have affected my work in a most negative manner. If only I had more help."

"I could help you. My mom always says she likes working better when I'm around," suggested Josh.

"She likes my help and Ellen's, too, you know," muttered Will.

"I never said she didn't like your help, but you know she likes me the best."

"She does not."

"She does so."

"Why do you say that?"

Josh gave him a knowing smile. "Because I'm the youngest. I'm the baby."

"You're only the baby by three minutes," said Ellen.

"That may be, but I'm still the baby. Mothers always love their babies the best."

"That's not true. Mom says she loves us all the same. We're all equal in the love department," said Will.

"You can think what you want, but I'm going to think what I want. I know Mom loves me the best. I can just tell."

"Whatever," scoffed Will.

Josh looked at Ben's uncle. "So what do you say, Mr. Zelenka? Can we be your helpers?" asked Josh.

Pepik appeared to be confused by this all. He let out a small cough, which quickly turned into an uncontrollable spasm of choking. "Why, I suppose," he said, his face all red as he struggled to catch his breath. "Help is always good."

"Thank you, Uncle Pepik. It will be nice to have some company. Shall I go find them some clothes?" asked Ben.

"Why, yes, my goodness. I suppose we can't have them working as they are now. That would be rather scandalous, don't you think?"

"I don't know about the scandalous part, Uncle, but everyone would stare at them."

"All right, then, perhaps they can borrow some of your things. Scrounge up whatever else they need from the neighbors."

"Thank you, Uncle. I'll be right back."

Ben dashed out the door and returned ten minutes later with a heap of clothing in his arms. He handed each of the boys a pair of short wool breeches, a baggy white shirt, some long, thin white socks, and a pair of scuffed leather shoes. Ellen received a matching shirt and skirt and a pair of shoes. Ben led them over to the cot in the corner and pulled a curtain around it. "You can change in here," he said, before wandering off to help his uncle.

"Thanks," said Ellen. She ducked behind the curtain.

Will lifted his clothing to his nose and took a sniff. "I'm not wearing this stuff," he whispered. "It smells like it hasn't been washed in years, and there are three holes in the socks alone."

"I like mine," said Josh. "Look, I even have a matching vest." He started putting on his new clothes, right on top of his boxer shorts and T-shirt.

Just then, Ellen popped out from behind the curtain, wearing a simple brown outfit made of heavy brown cloth. "Don't complain. Your stuff sure beats this. I hope I don't overheat in it."

Will went behind the curtain next. He emerged a few minutes later and stood there glumly, as if he had the weight of the world resting on his shoulders.

"What's the matter?" asked Ellen.

"I hate wearing other people's clothes. This baggy shirt is going to get in my way," he grumbled.

"Well, there's not much you can do about it, so you may as well try to make the best of it."

"Yes, Mother."

By now, Josh was completely dressed. He stood there with a smug grin on his face as he admired his new clothing. "Ben, this is great," he called out. "I especially like this vest, but there's just one problem."

"What's that?" said Ben, meandering over.

"These pants are really itchy. They're going to drive me crazy." He started to scratch his left hip, but the more he scratched, the worse he felt.

Ellen looked over to Will. "Count your blessings. It looks like Josh might be allergic to wool."

The kids assembled in a semicircle around Pepik. "Is everyone ready to begin?" he asked.

"Yes, Uncle," replied Ben.

"Then it's all settled. It is traditional that aspiring alchemists begin by doing vegetable work, but before you begin, you may join Benjamin. He'll be hiking out to the meadow to gather some wildflowers and horsetail. It is a most auspicious time, with the full moon and all."

"What's that got to do with anything?" asked Josh.

"At the full moon the sap is running high, and the plant is in its prime. This is important because the plant's vitality is in its stems and leaves. Benjamin will give you further instructions. Son, remember not to pick too much from any one spot. We must be grateful in our harvest."

"How far is the meadow?" asked Josh.

"A day's walk each way. If we leave now, we can pick tomorrow morning and be back by dawn on Sunday," said Ben.

A look of despair came over Will's face. "Did he say what I think he just said?"

Josh gave his brother a weak smile. "It's not that far. You'll be just fine."

— THREE —

GUNPOWDER

Ben was about to lead Josh, Will, and Ellen out the door when he suddenly stopped in his tracks and blocked the doorway. A distinguished looking man dressed in a finely tailored robe pushed his way past. He was over six feet tall, with long, pencil-thin arms and legs. His thick shock of short white hair matched his twirly moustache. Two enormous apricot-colored dogs, each the size of a loveseat, ambled along after him.

The dogs moved in closer until they were stepping on his toes. "Apollo, Zeus, down," he commanded. They looked up and gave him a look of total adoration but didn't move.

He tried again. "Down." The smaller of the two dogs responded with a deep woof. The man sighed and forced its back down until it was in a sitting position, and then repeated the process with the other dog.

Josh looked over to Ben. "What's that stuff dripping out of their mouths?" he whispered.

"It's drool. If you see them about to shake, get out of the way, fast."

Will took a few steps backwards. "I'm getting out of the way now. They might want to eat me."

"Nah, you wouldn't taste good. You're too skinny," said Josh.

Will gave him a dirty look.

"My new apprentices, this is our neighbor, Edward Scotta, commonly known as Scottie, and his dogs, Apollo and Zeus. They are quite safe. They accompany him wherever he goes," said Uncle Pepik.

Josh fumbled through layers of clothes until he reached his pajama shirt and pulled two dog biscuits out of his shirt pocket. He gave one of them a little lick. "Good. They're cheese and bacon flavored—Finnie's favorite. They'll love them."

Before he could walk over and give the dogs his treats, Zeus caught a whiff of the biscuits and lunged at him.

"Josh, watch out," shrieked Ellen.

Will hid behind Pepik's legs, trembling.

Even though he felt like running, Josh stood his ground. Zeus skidded to a stop in front of him and stood up on his hind legs, gently placing his paws on Josh's chest. He bent down, sniffed the hand holding the biscuit, then licked Josh's face with his big, wet tongue.

Josh cringed. "Okay, okay, that's enough. Here, take it, and stop licking me." Zeus dropped onto all fours and gently took the biscuit from Josh's hand before swallowing it in a single gulp. Then he stood back up on his hind legs and licked Josh's face again, covering it in slimy drool.

"All right, I get the picture. I know you like me. Back off." He tried to push Zeus away, but the dog wouldn't move.

Apollo slowly ambled over to Josh. "Oh, not you, too," he groaned. The dog hung his head and looked up at Josh with big, sad eyes. "Okay, here's your biscuit. Take it nice." Apollo slurped it out of his hand and walked back to Scottie. He slumped to the floor, dropped the biscuit between his front paws, and began delicately nibbling on it.

Josh was standing there, watching the dogs, when a chill ran up his spine. He looked up and discovered Scottie staring at him. He felt like Scottie's piercing blue eyes could see right through his skin and bones. A flash of recognition flickered through his head. *I've seen this guy before. He's the man from the picture on the wall!*

Scottie gave him a sinister smile. "Well, my, my. It appears my dogs have taken a liking to you. They are very good with children."

Josh cast him a wary glance. "How do you tell them apart?"

"Apollo is slightly bigger than Zeus, and he rarely leaves my side. Zeus is completely different; he's far more sociable. If you look carefully, you'll see his head is a bit darker."

"What kind of dogs are they?"

"English mastiffs, the finest breed in the world. What the lion is to the cat, the mastiff is to the dog." He let out an evil chuckle. "They have a violent past, you know—they were used for war. It is said that Caesar's favorite dog was a mastiff, and that the Kubla Khan kept a kennel of five thousand of them for hunting and battle."

Josh turned to his sister. "Imagine all the drool."

Ellen tried not to giggle.

With the dogs safely back at their master's side, Will summoned the courage to join his brother. "I've heard of mastiffs before, but I've never seen one until now. There was a mastiff on the Mayflower when it landed at Plymouth."

Apollo responded to this bit of information by letting out a thunderous burp. Everyone but Scottie burst out laughing. The poor dog hung his head in shame.

Scottie scowled, and their laughter quickly faded into an awkward silence. "So, Pepik, did more of your poor relations materialize on your doorstep overnight?" he asked.

"We're not relatives. We're training to be alchemists," announced Josh.

"It's a shame you didn't come see me first. You'd get much better training with me, you know."

Ben walked up to Scottie and placed his hands on his hips. "Leave them alone. They're here to help us, not you."

"Now, son, there is no need for hostility." Pepik grabbed his nephew by the shoulder and pulled him back. "We both work for the emperor, seeking the same common good."

Scottie smacked Pepik on the back. "You old fool! I am the only true alchemist in the emperor's employ, and you know it."

"Let's not start an argument now, neighbor. Time will reveal those who practice with integrity and those who are charlatans."

"What's a charlatan?" whispered Josh.

"A person who pretends they can do something that they really can't," replied Will.

"Oh."

Scottie turned his attention back to the boys. "What has Pepik taught you?" he asked.

"Actually, he hasn't taught us anything yet, but Ben told us that the purpose of alchemy is to create an elixir that turns metal into gold and makes anyone who drinks it immortal," answered Josh.

"And?"

"That's all."

"That's all? Pepik, you have been negligent in your teaching. How do you expect these young people to learn when you don't provide them with even the basic information?"

"Now, Scottie, we've only just begun. I've had very little time with my apprentices."

Scottie shook his head in disgust. "Children, if you wish to make the elixir of life, you should come work with me. Old Pepik has been on this journey a long time and has experienced much failure, but I, on the other hand, have mastered the laboratory techniques and almost perfected the elixir to the point where I can make mountains of gold." He rubbed his hands together and giggled with glee. "Imagine, I shall have the ability to possess whatever my heart desires."

He looked Josh and his siblings over from top to bottom once more. "I am always in need of assistants. Should you change your mind, you have a standing invitation to join me. If you have unlimited time and great patience, stick with old Pepik and his antiquated "moist" method. I hope he succeeds before he moves on to his heavenly reward."

"I'm not sparring with you today, Scottie. I've got too much to do." Pepik walked over to his furnace and started fiddling with the wood burning inside.

Scottie turned sharply and walked out the cottage door, bending down so he wouldn't bump his head. Apollo and Zeus trotted after him, their tails wagging. Just when it looked like he was gone, he poked his head back through the doorway and gave the children one final unnerving smile. "Remember my offer. You are welcome any time," he added, and then he disappeared.

"That guy sounds like he knows what he's doing. Maybe we should go with him," suggested Will.

"He gives me the creeps; and besides, I don't like the way he treated Ben and his uncle. I'd rather stay here until we know more," said Josh.

Ellen nodded in agreement. "Me, too. He said we could join him any time, so what's the hurry?"

Will folded his arms over his chest. "He sounds more confident. If it weren't for those dogs, I'd definitely go with him."

"Go ahead. I'm staying here," said Josh.

Will shrugged. "I'll stay for now, but I sure hope you're right."

Ben grabbed a basket and dropped in a half-eaten loaf of bread, a long piece of sausage, and a ball of cheese. He handed Josh the basket and lifted two glass containers off the workbench. He was walking over to his uncle, expecting to give him a quick hug before heading out the door, when Pepik excitedly held up a jar of prickly seeds.

"Look! Here it is. I just unearthed the *Equisetum arvense*, or 'horse-tail' as Ben likes to call it. There is no need for you to go to the meadow. The four of you can help me pulverize it these other ingredients instead. Get down the mortars and pestles."

Will breathed a sigh of relief, but Ben, who knew what was coming, looked disappointed. He handed Josh and Will each a small bowl and a wooden tool with a round end.

Josh examined his. "What do we do with these?"

"You put seeds in it," said Ben, holding up his bowl, "and then you use the round end of the pestle to grind them up. See, like this."

He poured some of the horsetail into his bowl and turned it with quick, efficient movements until the seeds were ground into a fine dust.

"This can't be too hard." Josh dumped some of the horsetail into his bowl and started grinding. Will followed suit.

"But what about me? What am I supposed to do? Just sit here and watch?" asked Ellen.

"New apprentices always think this is easier than it looks. Just give them a minute. They'll be begging for your help," whispered Ben.

Josh worked hard, deep in concentration, pressing the pestle into the seeds with all his might. After several minutes, he inspected the contents of his bowl, and held it out for Ben to see. "Look, I'm done. That wasn't so bad. I can tell I'm going to be good at this alchemy stuff."

"It's not fine enough yet." Ben showed him the seeds he had been grinding. "Mine are half the size of yours, and I'm not nearly done yet."

"Great. This is going to take me all day," muttered Josh under his breath. Suddenly a big smile flashed across his face. He handed his mortar and pestle to his sister. "Here you go. It's your turn."

Ellen and Ben exchanged a knowing smile. A minute later, Uncle Pepik walked over to check on their progress.

"This is very tedious work," said Ellen.

"It most certainly is, which leads me right to our first lesson: the spiritual component of alchemy. Benjamin, I noticed you neglected to meditate on the task at hand before you began."

Benjamin hung his head. "I'm sorry, Uncle. It's just that I hate that part. It seems so . . . I don't know . . . So useless."

"Turning our thoughts to our heavenly Father is never a useless endeavor, my dear boy. Apprentices, before you do anything in the laboratory, it is important that you stop, bow your heads, think about what you are doing and why, and offer up a silent prayer for the gifts of creation you are about to use."

"I can understand the prayer part, but why do you have to stop and think about what you're doing before you do it?" asked Josh.

"Alchemy is a very complicated endeavor. It requires the intelligence of the heart as well as of the mind. When we calm our hearts and think about what we're doing, we are more likely to hear God's voice as we work. I believe that as an alchemist grows spiritually, the success of his work will increase. A person will not be able to receive the secret knowledge if their heart is not right."

Will's eyes lit up. "What sort of 'secret knowledge' are we talking about?"

"Over the centuries, the instructions for our work have been written in a kind of code which uses double encryption. First, it relies on a variety of pictures using special symbols. Drawings of gods and heroes, monsters and fairies, and real and imaginary animals are used to describe our work and the way our ingredients interact with one another. From there, the directions are further outlined in a kind of labyrinth. Puns and anagrams are used to bury our truths in second and third meanings; important words are split and recombined to fool the uninitiated, and the steps are often listed in the wrong order to confuse the reader. One procedure might be broken up and scattered between several chapters of a book or between many books. On top of this, false recipes are often inserted into the directions. Only those who have spent their lives studying alchemy are able to attain true understanding. Even then alchemists disagree frequently on how the Great Work should be carried out."

"That is why our motto is *oro, lege, relege, labora, et invenis*," added Ben. "That's Latin for 'Pray, read, reread, work, and you shall find.'" Pepik nodded approvingly.

"So you mix up your directions so that people who haven't studied alchemy won't be able to understand them?" said Josh.

"Exactly. My, you are a bright lad."

Josh made sure his brother and sister were looking at him, thumped his thumb against his chest, and nodded and smiled.

"Alchemists have a code of conduct, some of it spoken and some unspoken, which governs our work. Albertus Magnus wrote out an eight-point code in *Libellus De Alchemia*. Would you like to hear the eight points?" asked Pepik.

"Sure."

"One: We must not reveal our secrets. Two: We work in private. Three: We do our work during the most suitable hours of the day, so that we'll have greater success. Four: We must be patient and persevere to the end. We cannot give up. Five: We must operate by the precepts of our art—"

"—What does that mean?" interrupted Josh.

"It means that we do things properly—we don't take shortcuts. As for the rest, all our vessels are to be made of glass; we should not demonstrate our abilities before royalty; and finally, we should not practice alchemy unless we have enough money, because if our funds run out, all our efforts will be wasted."

"Do you follow all of these rules?"

"As much as I am able. I don't always have a choice."

"I still don't understand why it has to be such a big secret," maintained Will.

"Well, now, stop and think about it. If you had the ability to turn any metal into gold, giving you the potential for unlimited riches, and if by drinking this elixir, you could live for two or three hundred years or maybe forever, don't you think people would be flocking to you, begging for just a sip?"

"I suppose."

"And once they had a little bit, do you think they would ever be satisfied?" Pepik shook his head. "When they ran out, they would be waiting on your doorstep, pleading with you to give them more."

"I guess that would be a problem," agreed Will.

"You have no idea, my friend, of the madness that grips men when the thought of this substance, this *elixir of life*, this *philosopher's stone*, is placed before them. This entire street, Golden Lane, is funded by our mad emperor, Rudolph II, in the hope that one of us will discover it. His spies are about constantly, monitoring our progress and watching for even the tiniest glimmer of success."

"Spies? You were serious. Wow. This is a big deal," exclaimed Josh.

"It most certainly is."

"Why did you decide to become an alchemist?" asked Ellen.

"I have been studying alchemy since I was a young lad, probably about your brothers' age, in the hope it would help me grow closer to God. Our heavenly Father often speaks to me as I work here in the laboratory. As my ability to transform metal increases, so does the transformation of my heart."

Will gave him a skeptical glance. "What makes you think you can transform metal?"

"Let me give you a quick science lesson. There are seven different metals: gold, silver, iron, copper, tin, lead, and mercury, and they form underground when mercury and sulphur combine. If there is more mercury than sulphur, you get tin and lead, the more meltable metals. If there is more sulphur than mercury, copper and iron, the harder metals, will result."

"Gold results when mercury and sulphur combine in the exact proportions," prompted Ben.

"That is correct, son. Over time, nature will turn all metals into gold underground, but it may take thousands of years. That is why I am trying to create the philosopher's stone."

"It speeds up the whole process," added Ben.

"Can you excuse us for a minute?" said Will. He grabbed Josh and Ellen by the arm and hauled them to the other side of the room.

"What are you doing?" asked Josh. He jerked his arm away.

"We've got a problem here. There are way more than seven metals in the Periodic Table of the Elements, and I'm quite sure they aren't turning into gold underground," whispered Will.

"He's right. This doesn't go with what we learned in science last year," mumbled Josh.

"Don't say anything. We can't just barge in here and tell them that everything they think is wrong. They wouldn't believe us," said Ellen.

"Are you sure?" asked Josh.

"Positive." She walked back to Pepik. "I'm sorry, sir, we didn't mean to interrupt."

He took this as an invitation to continue. "I like the way that alchemy explains life. It may be a great mystery from ancient times that was almost lost, but it still makes sense today. It recognizes that we reap what we sow, that our life is a preparation for death, and that this life on earth is only one part of our journey."

Josh furrowed his brow. "I've never heard of any great mystery before. What is it?"

"My goodness, lad, you are full of questions, aren't you? It's good to be curious. Don't ever lose your longing for knowledge. It will serve you well your entire life."

Will rolled his eyes. "He obviously doesn't know about your marks at school."

Josh stuck out his tongue.

"Legend has it that alchemy originated in a lost civilization that was destroyed by a great flood thousands of years ago. This lost civilization, sometimes called the 'Sons of Reflected Light,' passed their knowledge along to the ancient Egyptians, who used it to build their great pyramids," declared Pepik.

"They wrote these directions on an emerald plate—" said Ben.

"—Which was supposedly found by Sarah, the wife of Abraham, in a cave in Hebron. Others say that the traditions were handed down to Moses during his time in the royal palace when he was trained in all the wisdom of Egypt."

Ellen let out a big yawn. "Oops, sorry," she said, blushing.

Pepik looked almost as embarrassed as she did. "I must apologize. I have gone on rather long. My passion for my work sometimes gets the better of me."

"Can I ask just one more question?" said Josh.

"Of course."

"If you made the elixir and turned a bunch of metal into gold, what would you do with all the money?"

Pepik didn't hesitate for even a second. "I would give it to the church. The money wouldn't do me much good. There's nothing I need."

"Really? That's not what I thought you'd say."

"Good. I'm glad I surprised you. Now back to your grinding, please."

Josh worked away with his mortar and pestle. When his hand and arm began to ache, he tried to pass Ellen his equipment, but Will had beat him to it. He wandered around until he found a clear space on the floor on the other side of the room and sat down. When Ellen looked up and spotted him sitting there looking rather dejected, she walked over and joined him.

"What's wrong?" she asked as she dropped to the floor.

"There's something that's really bugging me," he replied quietly, so only she could hear.

"What?"

"How come everyone knows so much except for me? Will knew all about those dogs, and Ben knows about alchemy. I feel like I don't know anything."

"People always learn about the things they really care about. That's why Dad knows so much about woodworking and Mom about painting. When you're really into something, you remember what you've learned more easily."

"That still doesn't explain how Will knew about those dogs. He doesn't even like dogs, except for Finnegan, of course."

"Will's an exception to the rule."

"That's nice, but I still feel dumb."

"Josh, you're not dumb. You just know about different things than Will. Think about everything you know about basketball. I don't know anyone else who knows the statistics for every player, the shots and strategies, and whatever else it is that you know."

Josh perked up. "You're right. I do know a lot about something. If you ever want to know anything about jump shots, I'm your man."

"Try to remember that when you're feeling down."

"Okay." He gave her a big smile. "Ready to do some of my grinding?"

Josh walked across the room to Pepik's table and picked up an ancient book. He slowly turned its pages, studying the strange drawings. There were people in cloaks pointing to smoking pots, suns and moons with faces surrounded by blazing fires, tall flasks with three-headed birds inside, and countless dragons and snakes. Once he'd paged through the entire book, he walked back to the workbench where Ellen and Ben were grinding. Will was standing beside them, taking a break, inspecting Pepik's jars of herbs and potions.

Josh reached over his brother's shoulder and lifted a jar labeled "saltpeter" off the shelf. "I wonder what 'saltpeter' is? What do you think it's used for?"

"Whatever you do, don't open it. If you mix it with sulfur and charcoal, you make gunpowder," warned Will.

"Cool! Do you have any idea how much you need to put in?"

"You use seventy-five percent saltpeter, fourteen percent charcoal, and eleven percent sulfur." Will looked at him over the top of his glasses. "You wouldn't be thinking about making any, would you?"

"Me? Make gunpowder? I'd never do that," said Josh, his fingers crossed behind his back. "How did you learn that? Never mind, don't tell me. You probably read it in a book."

Josh waited until Will had wandered off and the others were busy. Eventually Will became engrossed in one of Uncle Pepik's alchemy books at the other side of the room, and Ellen and Ben were standing with Pepik, helping him gather ingredients from his apothecary chest. When Josh was sure no one was looking, he grabbed an empty bowl, pried open the container of saltpeter, and poured a good-sized pile into the bowl. Next he added a little mound of charcoal and a big sprinkle of sulfur, and then he quickly mixed the three ingredients together.

Will put down his book and started to walk back, so Josh quickly pulled a tissue out from under the waistband of his boxers. It was one of those extra strong ones his mom kept on hand for his dad, the ones he wasn't supposed to use. He poured a handful of the mixture into it, jammed the bulky Kleenex into his boxers, and shoved the bowl of gunpowder to the back of the workbench. By the time Will reached him, Josh was standing there, whistling, as he pretended to examine a large egg perched on the shelf.

"Hey, Uncle Pepik, what bird did this come from?" he said in a loud voice, holding up the egg.

Pepik looked up from his work. "It's a bezoar."

"What's that?" asked Will.

"A calcium deposit from the intestine of an ibex."

Josh almost dropped it. He quickly put it back. "That's disgusting."

"Do you think we'll be done grinding soon? I can't do any more; my hand is killing me," whined Will.

"I'll do yours," volunteered Josh, eager to leave the workbench and his strange concoction behind.

"Let me see how you're doing," said Uncle Pepik. He inspected the contents of the mortar. The seeds were ground into a fine dust. "You're almost there. Just a few more minutes."

Pepik glanced at his workbench. He picked up Josh's bowl. "Hmm. Somehow this seems to have moved out of place."

A feeling of panic shot through Josh's stomach.

"I don't remember mixing this. I wonder what it is," he mumbled.

Great, now I'm really in trouble, thought Josh.

Will came over to take a closer look. "It looks like charcoal."

Pepik lifted the bowl to his nose and took a big whiff. "You're right, there does appear to be some charcoal in here, but there's something else." He stirred the powder with his wrinkled finger. "Hmm. This is most unusual."

"Let me see," said Will. He took a deep sniff too. "I don't know what it is."

"Ben, did you make this?" asked Pepik, holding the bowl above his head so Ben could see it from the other side of the room.

"It wasn't me, Uncle. It's probably something you mixed up yesterday. You often leave stuff lying around."

Josh slowly exhaled. "I owe you one," he muttered under his breath. Will gave Josh an uneasy glance.

Pepik shook the bowl, causing the powder to shift from one side to the other. "You're probably right. Oh, well, it's no good to me now." He walked over to the furnace, opened the door, and threw the contents of the bowl at the open flames before Josh could protest.

A plume of white smoke poured out of the furnace, filling the room. Pepik stood there, as still as a statue, staring at the furnace, as if he couldn't believe what was happening.

"Quick, we've got to get out of here," yelled Josh. He started herding everyone toward the door. "Uncle Pepik, come!"

The five of them escaped from the cottage seconds before the furnace exploded, blowing out the windows and flinging the door, hinges and all, onto the street. Soon the entire building was engulfed in flames.

Pepik's neighbors quickly organized a fire brigade. Bucket after bucket of water was thrown onto the blazing cottage. Fortunately, the neighboring houses were spared; the only damage to them was a thick layer of ash.

Once the fire was completely out, Pepik stood in front of the charred shell of his home. "I cannot believe this is happening again. It must be a bad dream. I'm getting too old to start over. All of my work is destroyed, gone forever."

He was scanning the ruins when a glimmer of hope flashed across his face. He gingerly tiptoed through the swampy mess, swept away a thick layer of wet ash from the floor with his foot, and carefully lifted a singed floorboard. Falling to his knees, he lifted out three leather-bound books and clutched them to his chest, weeping.

"My precious books, they survived. Perhaps there is hope after all."

— FOUR —

STRANGE HAPPENINGS

Pepik rubbed his round belly as he surveyed his new cottage. "My goodness, who would have thought that something so good could have come out of something so bad? In my wildest dreams I never thought I'd get to work in a laboratory like this. Everything is new, and of such superior quality. And to think we're only six doors down from where we were before!"

"You mean you didn't know that this empty lab was here?" asked Will, fingering one of the new glass flasks stacked in a tidy row on the workbench.

"Many of the residents of Golden Lane have been speculating as to the purposes of this building, but I try to avoid their never-ending gossip. The comings and goings of the emperor's workers drives Scottie in particular into quite a frenzy." Pepik smiled to himself. At the knock on the door, his joyful expression vanished. "I was hoping he would give me some time to resume my work. I don't need more trouble."

"Uncle Pepik, Scottie has half the emperor's henchmen in his back pocket. He keeps a closer eye on every single alchemist in the city than the emperor himself. I don't expect you'll get much of a break," cautioned Ben.

"We shall see," mumbled Pepik as he shuffled across the floor.

Pepik opened the door. Two guards, dressed in red and black uniforms with braided gold trim, stood outside the tiny cottage, the tips of their hats higher than the roofline. The gold buttons on their jackets, embossed with the emperor's royal crest, gleamed in the sunlight.

One of the guards gave him a friendly nod. "What can I do for you gentlemen today?" asked Pepik.

"The commander instructed us to ensure that all your needs have been met," said the older guard.

"This lab is magnificent. It shall be a delight to work here."

"Very well." He cocked his head to one side and studied the children standing at the back of the room. Josh was casually leaning against the workbench, watching, when an anxious feeling seized his heart.

"Who are your visitors?" asked the guard.

Pepik turned around. "Oh . . . Them . . . Well . . . They turned up the other day with Benjamin and have become my apprentices."

"What is their experience?"

"I am uncertain. They know little—it is almost as if alchemy is unknown in their land," he mused. "This laboratory, though, is truly magnificent." Pepik swept his arms back to take in the entire room and its contents. "Please pass my thanks along to your commander and His Majesty as well."

The guard turned to his partner. A private conversation ensued. They looked at Josh every few seconds, as if they expected him to bolt out the door. Eventually they asked Pepik to join them outside. He followed them out to the narrow lane and closed the door behind him.

"What's going on? Why did they keep looking at me?" fretted Josh.

Will crossed his arms over his chest and gave Josh a withering look. "Do you think it might have something to do with the fact that you just blew up a lab?"

"I didn't exactly blow it up. Uncle Pepik's the one who threw the gunpowder into the fire."

"Oh, so now it's his fault? You made the gunpowder, you didn't tell

Uncle Pepik what it was when he asked about it, and you didn't stop him from throwing it into the fire, and it's his fault?"

"At least I got everyone out in time."

"And it's a good thing, because it could have been a lot worse."

"Rudolph's spies are always on the lookout for information to bring to His Majesty. You might be in a lot of trouble," said Ben.

A few minutes later the door opened and Pepik wandered back into the room with a quirky grin on his face.

"Uncle, why are you smiling?" asked Ben.

"It appears that our new apprentice has made quite an impression. Josh's explosion is the talk of the town, which is quite unusual as explosions happen here all the time. The reason I was smiling is because the emperor believes Josh possesses some sort of secret knowledge that has not existed here before. Who knows? Maybe His Majesty is right. I shall add this to the list of things I do not understand."

Pepik popped a cap onto his nearly bald head. "I'm stepping out for a few minutes. The cupboards are bare, and the dinner hour will be upon us shortly. Familiarize yourselves with the lab while I'm gone. When I return, we shall eat."

Pepik had been gone just a few minutes when Scottie burst into the room. Apollo and Zeus bounded in after him. He immediately spotted Ben standing next to a bookshelf, carefully arranging a set of rare alchemy texts.

"Aargh, it is true!" he roared. "This was supposed to be my lab, not my ne'er-do-well neighbor's. Just one more step and I would have completed the transmutation and gained this lab as my prize."

"My uncle's not a ne'er-do-well. He's more dedicated to the Great Work than you are," declared Ben.

"Then tell me of his successes."

Ben turned beet red; even his ears were blazing. "That's not a fair question and you know it."

Scottie gave him a sly grin. "And why would that be? Perhaps you should enlighten your newfound friends regarding your uncle's abilities. After all, the proof of the pudding is under the crust."

Ben glared at him but didn't say a word.

"Well, then, children, I believe it would be in your best interests to know that your teacher, Pepik Zelenka, has never actually completed a transmutation. In fact, his laboratory conveniently burns down every time he claims to be getting close."

"It's probably just a coincidence," said Josh, feeling even guiltier for his part in the morning's fire. "Uncle Pepik told us that fires happen here all the time."

"That's one way of looking at it."

"What do you mean by that?" asked Will.

"Perhaps Pepik's lab conveniently burns down because he's afraid people will discover he's a fraud."

"My uncle's not a fraud!" exclaimed Ben.

A hush fell over the room as Josh, Will, and Ellen processed this information.

Ben paced back and forth. "Don't listen to him. He doesn't know what he's talking about. He's never done a transmutation, either. They're very rare, you know. My uncle's one of the kindest people you could ever meet. Scottie's lying." He nervously ran his hand through his unruly mop of hair.

Scottie walked over to him and placed his hand on Ben's shoulder. Ben jerked away, but Scottie ignored his reaction and pulled the boy to his side. "Ben, dear Ben," he said, in a quiet, gentle voice, "I would never, never question your uncle's kindness. I agree completely that he is one of the finest men on this lane, perhaps even in this city."

Ben looked up at him; his eyes gleamed with unshed tears. "Really?"

"Of course. Why, your uncle was one of the first people to welcome me when I arrived last year. Don't you remember the way he invited me into your home, fed me, and even let me sleep in his own bed until I made my own arrangements? Why, he even tolerated my dogs, and you know how much of an interruption they can be."

"That's right. I remember when both of them had an accident that first night. The puddle covered the entire floor." Ben smiled at the memory.

"Yes, they were a bit anxious from the move. How many people would tolerate that, I ask you? As I said, your uncle is a fine, fine man."

"Thank you."

"But that doesn't change the fact that we all want to be on a winning team. Each one of us wants to create the elixir and enjoy the benefits it will bring, or we wouldn't be here. I can tell you, without a doubt, that you are more likely to achieve this if you work with me."

Ben turned to the others. "Don't believe anything he says. It's all nonsense."

"Whoa, just a minute here. I'll decide that for myself. I want to know all our options," interrupted Will.

"But I trust Uncle Pepik," said Josh.

"That's right," added Ben. "We're working with my uncle."

"I want to hear what Scottie has to say. There's nothing wrong with that," insisted Will.

An enormous scowl settled on Ben's face. His eyebrows sank down and his lips were pinched tight. "Don't believe a word he says," he pouted.

Will rolled his eyes and turned back to Scottie. "What makes you think you can do better than Ben's uncle?"

"The answer to your question is quite lengthy. I believe I shall sit down." Scottie took a seat on one of Pepik's new chairs. Apollo and Zeus lay down on either side of him. Apollo had just settled in, her head resting on his foot, when suddenly she lurched to one side. A horrible smell filled the room.

Josh began to giggle. When the smell of rotten eggs reached Ellen, she madly fanned the air in front of her with one hand and plugged her nose with the other.

Apollo lay her chin on the floor and gave them a dejected look. Scottie reached down and patted her on the head. "It's all right, old girl. No more sausage for you tonight." He gestured to the children. "Come, sit down."

The four of them sat down on the floor in front of him. Josh, Will, and Ellen looked up expectantly. Ben sat there with a scowl still etched on his face.

"Now, to get back to your question, I can outperform Pepik's alchemy in any given situation. I studied with some of the best adepts across the continent, who had amazing abilities I could only dream of."

Scottie leaned back into his chair and stretched out his legs. "I began my studies with Cheng Yang in Asia. He possessed a 'Grand-Concealment' amulet. After wearing it for ten days, he could disappear by wheeling to the left and reappear by wheeling to the right. He also had the ability to transform his body into various shapes. I saw him turn into a tree on one occasion. It was quite a sight to behold. He achieved his greatest success, however, after he drank his final elixir. Imagine my surprise when he sprouted magnificent feathered wings, rose effortlessly off the ground, and disappeared into the morning sky. I never did see him again," he added wistfully.

Josh let out a little cough.

Will and Ellen looked over to him.

He twirled his finger beside his head and mouthed the word "cuckoo."

Ellen shot him a dirty look.

"After my time in Asia, I traveled to India, where I studied under the Siddhas. They were also able to fly, not by using wings, but by placing a special substance in their mouths that gave them the power of flight. The elixirs they prepared also gave them immense strength and supernatural vision."

"Where can I get some of that stuff?" asked Josh.

Scottie gave him a condescending smile. "It is only available to advanced adepts. The final stop in my journey was Egypt. I spent many days at the Edfu temple reading the remarkable inscriptions carved on its walls. It was there that I finally accepted the truth that alchemy was brought to us by messengers from an ancient civilization that perished during a great catastrophe. Much of their teaching has been lost over the centuries, but the Egyptian temple priests freely shared their knowledge with me."

"What kind of knowledge are we talking about?"

Scottie leaned in close. "Knowledge of the immortals," he whispered.

Josh glanced over at Ben. The scowl on his face was gone, and he sat there, almost holding his breath, as he waited for Scottie to continue.

Scottie's eyes shifted back and forth across the room. "I think it is safe to speak of this, but you must promise never to repeat what I am about to tell you. Understand?"

They nodded in agreement.

"The Egyptians possessed the ability to make a unique elixir. The amount of cinnabar had to be exactly right, but if it were, the person who drank their magical potion would become immortal. If they drank half a dose, they could live forever in this world, and if they drank a full dose, they could go right up to heaven. It was their choice."

"What's cinnabar?" asked Will.

"Would you like to see some?"

He nodded.

Scottie solemnly pulled a handkerchief out of his pocket and carefully opened it. There, resting in the palm of his hand, was a mound of reddish orange powder, about the size of a pecan. "I watched a temple priest work with this. He sprinkled a tiny bit of it onto some mercury, heated it, and when he lifted the lid of the container, there was a nugget of gold inside exactly the same weight as the original mercury."

"Why don't you demonstrate it for us right now?" suggested Ben.

Scottie jumped to his feet. The dogs sat up and stretched. "My goodness, time has gotten away from me again. I must be getting back to my laboratory."

The wonder on Ben's face quickly vanished.

"If I stay even a second longer, my experiments will surely suffer. I need to complete them today, for then I can go to the emperor and request more funding. Sometimes I think there must be a hole in my pocket, because money seems to slip through my fingers faster than I receive it." He carefully folded up his handkerchief, put it back in his pocket, and walked out the door with Apollo and Zeus trotting behind.

"He always leaves when he's asked to demonstrate his techniques. I wonder how long it will take for the emperor to figure out that he's all talk and no action," said Ben.

Josh stood up. "I can barely dream of some of the stuff he talked about. Imagine, sprouting wings and flying. That would be awesome. I wish I could do that."

"Are you serious?" asked Ellen.

"Of course. Think about it: You could go wherever you wanted, whenever you wanted. I could fly over to my friends' houses. That would really shock them."

"Then why don't we go work with Scottie? Maybe he could make you some of the elixir," suggested Will.

Josh shook his head. "That would be wrong. We're supposed to be here with Ben and Uncle Pepik. I just know it."

"But nothing much is happening around here," maintained Will.

"I know, but I'm not going anywhere. I'm staying here with Ben. He's the first person we found. That means he's the one we're supposed to be with."

"I agree. I really like Uncle Pepik. He might not be a big talker, but I think we should stick with him," said Ellen.

"I guess I'm outnumbered," grumbled Will.

"You can go with Scottie if you want," said Josh.

"I'll stay with you guys for now, but I sure hope this is the right decision." He glanced over at Ben. "No offense, okay?"

"Trust me, you're doing the right thing," said Ben. "I'd better load up the furnace before my uncle gets back. He'll want to start his distillations as soon as possible." He took some coal out of a wicker basket, opened the lower door of the furnace tower, and carefully arranged it inside.

"How do you know how much coal to put in?" asked Will.

"That depends on what kind of fire we need. It's important to get just the right amount of heat, which can be quite tricky."

"Do you measure the temperature?"

"No, we just build the fire in different ways. I'll start today with a common fire. My uncle will probably want a rotational fire by this evening."

"A what?"

"A common fire is a fire at the bottom of the furnace—just your normal everyday fire. A rotational fire is one that gives strong steady heat and is kept lit for however long the distillation takes."

"Oh."

"My favorite one is the philosophical fire; some people call it the secret fire. It . . ." Ben's voice trailed off as Uncle Pepik entered the room, his arms loaded with bread, cheese, and a slab of meat.

"Benjamin! Where is your head, dear boy? You know the rules governing our knowledge. It is not to be shared with the uninitiated, and certainly not by someone as new to the discipline as yourself." He shook his finger at his nephew. "Please, son, you must keep our confidences or you shall be no better than Scottie. I will teach our new friends the necessary knowledge once they are further along. That is my responsibility, not yours."

Ben hung his head in shame. "Sorry, Uncle. It won't happen again."

The five of them were eating their supper when someone knocked on the door. "Not again," grumbled Ben. He grabbed another piece of sausage and stuffed it in his mouth before he strolled across the room and opened the door.

The emperor's two guards were back. When Pepik spotted them, he jumped to his feet, almost tipping the table in the process. "My goodness, more official visitors," he blustered as he scurried over. "What brings you here this time?"

"The emperor has requested an audience with your guests," said one of the guards.

"Oh, my, this is quite unusual. They are mere children. Why does he wish to speak with them?"

The guard shrugged his shoulders. "He didn't say. Bring them at once."

Pepik gave the kids a minute to tidy themselves up, and then Josh, Will, and Ellen followed him and Ben down Golden Lane. They wound around several corners until they reached a broader street. A new section of the city spread out before them. Multi-story stone buildings with red tile roofs rose up on either side of the street. Josh was so excited that he skipped down the wide cobblestone street, chanting, "We're going to see the king, we're going to see the king," in a singsong voice.

Uncle Pepik gave him a curious look.

"Don't worry. He always acts kind of strange when he's excited," explained Will.

"Where is the king's castle?" sang Josh.

"We're in the castle right now," replied Pepik.

"We are?"

"Yes. Golden Lane is in the northeast end of it. It's just a tiny part, you know."

Josh looked around, his mouth hanging open. He suddenly began to appreciate how big Prague castle actually was. It included Golden Lane, the huge buildings with long rows of windows that surrounded them on all four sides, and a spectacular building right in the center of it all. The huge structure rose up in the midst of the walls, its tall spires appearing to reach for the clouds. Its height, along with its swirls and curls and peaks and stained glass, caused it to completely dominate everything around it.

"Whoa, look at that," exclaimed Josh. "Is that where that the king lives?"

Uncle Pepik chuckled. "No, that is St. Vitus's Cathedral. Follow me. His Majesty lives in the royal palace," he said, pointing to a building on their left.

"But it looks like all the other buildings. Shouldn't the king live in something more like that cathedral?"

"I assure you, the emperor's living quarters are quite grand. He is not suffering."

"Uncle Pepik, is there anything we need to know before we meet him?" asked Ellen.

"Yes, I have a few words of caution for you. Actually, I don't expect you will actually 'meet' the emperor. He often summons people to see him and then decides not to speak with them after all. But if you do see him, be extraordinarily polite. Don't speak to him unless he speaks to you first."

"What do you mean, we might not see him? You made us walk all this way for nothing?" grumbled Will.

"The emperor has become very peculiar over the years. He is deathly afraid of people and has not been seen in public for months now. It is said that he speaks to only a few trusted servants, and he never smiles. He only goes out at night, and even then, only if he's wearing a dark cloak that completely obscures him."

"If he's so afraid of people, why did he ask to see us?" asked Ellen.

"That question confounds me as well. To be perfectly honest, I'm not sure, my dear."

"I think it's obvious. We're important, that's why he wants to see us. It's not every day you get three visitors who time traveled from another country," declared Josh.

"You, 'important'? You've got to be kidding," snapped Will.

Josh whacked him on the arm. "In the past two months I've talked with a shaman who was the head of his village; two lords, one who was almost as rich as the Queen of England; and now Rudy wants to see me. Hah!"

"It's His Majesty Rudolph II to you, stupid." Will gave Uncle Pepik an apologetic glance. "Sorry about my brother. I didn't realize he was so important. Apparently, leaders around the world are desperate to speak with him, probably because of his great brilliance."

"What can I say?" said Josh, totally missing Will's sarcasm. "People want to see me. It must be because I'm so great."

"Or maybe it's because God is at work," observed Ellen softly.

Both boys fell silent at that humbling thought.

The guards in front of the palace greeted Pepik with a curt nod and ushered them inside. They were barely in the door when Josh plugged his nose. "It smells like mothballs or something."

Will gulped. "This doesn't feel right. I need to get out of here."

"Quit being so scared. Relax. Everything will be just fine."

As they traveled down the hall, Josh peeked through a doorway. It opened into a small sitting room. Several candles were glowing in the crystal chandelier. Light sparkled off its crystals, illuminating the boarded-up windows, the rugs covered in muddy footprints, and the furniture smothered in a thick layer of dust. Large paintings of what appeared to be kings and queens hung on the walls in elaborate gold frames.

After climbing three flights of stairs, they walked down another long hallway decorated with more paintings, fancy carved tables that held a variety of knickknacks, glass-fronted display cases, and the occasional overstuffed chair. A candle burned every fifteen steps or so, barely providing enough light for them to navigate. At the end of the corridor, a thick wooden door was flanked by two of the emperor's guards.

"Ben and I have to leave you here; the guards will take you in to see His Majesty. We'll be waiting outside. Remember what I told you—mind your manners—and everything will be fine," said Uncle Pepik.

"But . . . but . . . but I thought you were staying with us," stammered Will.

Josh moved closer to Pepik. "I don't want to go without you. It's creepy."

"You'll be fine. We'll see you shortly." One of the guards escorted Pepik and Ben away, and the other one entered the room to see if the emperor was ready.

"I have a bad feeling about this," moaned Will.

"You always get these bad feelings, and nothing ever happens," replied Josh with more confidence than he actually felt.

"Whatever you do, don't touch anything, okay?" warned Ellen.

"What? Me? I never touch anything," said Josh.

"Yeah, right."

He frowned. "I'll try not to."

"You have to do better than try. Just don't."

Josh turned his attention to the artwork and bric-a-brac nearby. A tall case held a variety of strange objects: a long curved white horn, several animal skulls, and the complete skeleton of a huge snake. A life-sized painting of a man made of vegetables hung on the wall next to the door. It was the strangest thing Josh had ever seen. The face had a pear for a nose; peapod eyelids; cobs of corn for ears; and apples, grapes, cherries, and stems of wheat for hair.

Josh was studying the picture, wondering whom it depicted, when he saw its eyes move from side to side. He gasped and jumped back, landing on top of Will's feet.

Will pushed him away. "Get off! You're hurting me."

"The eyes of that painting just moved. Someone's watching us," whispered Josh.

Will and Ellen looked up at the painting. "You've been watching too many scary movies. It looks perfectly normal to me, or as normal as a person made of fruit and vegetables could ever look," said Ellen.

The muffled sound of a thud and scurrying feet caused all three of them to jump.

"What was that?" asked Will, his voice quaking. He clutched his arms against his chest, trying not to shake.

"It's probably just a mouse. Old buildings like this are usually full of mice," said Ellen, trying to reassure herself as much as her brothers.

A second later the doorknob slowly turned, there was a brief pause, and then the door jerked open. The guard stepped out. "The emperor will see you now," he gruffly proclaimed.

— FIVE —

THE TOWER

CRBRBRCRCRBRBRCRCRBRBRCRCRBRBR

The minute Josh stepped through the doorway, everyhing felt wrong. Maybe Will's bad feelings were right. It was as if an invisible sinister cloud hovered in the air, just below the ceiling.

The curtains had been pulled shut, leaving the room in darkness, except for the flicker of light from four candles. One candle burned in an iron candelabra on a table in the center of the room, and three others burned in sconces on the walls.

Josh looked around in amazement, for the moment forgetting about the emperor. He had never been in a room so crammed with stuff before. It was like Pepik's cottage, but a hundred times worse. Every single table, shelf, ledge, cabinet, and chair was covered in layers of junk.

He walked over to one of the tables. A musical clock decorated with hunting scenes hung on the wall above it, its quiet ticking providing the only noise in the tomb-like room. "What's this?" he asked the guard, picking up a smoothly polished cup.

"That's a chalice made of rhinoceros horn. It's used for boiling poisonous potions."

"Oh. That's pretty weird." Josh moved to the next item that caught his attention and let his fingers trail over a plant root shaped like a little man, resting on a soft velvet cushion.

Will and Ellen scurried over to their brother. "When I said, 'don't touch anything' I meant it!" hissed Ellen.

"But there's stuff everywhere. I can't take two steps without bumping into the furniture." Josh tried to back up, but it was a struggle. "They should clean this place up. It's a mess."

He cupped his hand under his armpit and lowered his arm with a jerk, producing a rude noise. "Hey, guys, I think Apollo and Zeus are in here!"

Will giggled nervously, but Ellen was not impressed. She cuffed him on the shoulder. "Smarten up!"

He looked away, embarrassed, and then returned his gaze to the emperor's treasures.

The guard, apparently deciding to act as a tour guide, pointed to a beautiful bracelet. "This is made of gallstones—"

"Yuck!" whispered Ellen.

"—and these two nails are from Noah's ark. That iron chair holds whoever sits in it prisoner. Come here," he commanded.

"I'm not going anywhere near that chair," insisted Will.

"No, over here," said the guard, pointing to another table. It was covered in an assortment of shells, statues, coins, clay figurines, spectacles, turtle shells, and coconuts. He picked up a lump of dirt. "The emperor believes this is from the soil God used to create Adam." He raised his eyebrows and gave the children a doubtful smile.

A bell rang from somewhere down the hall. "His Majesty will be with you shortly. Whatever you do, don't touch his belongings." The guard strode out of the room, firmly closing the door behind him.

A quiet creak caught their attention. Josh turned to the door. There was no one there. He heard some quiet shuffling and realized the sound was coming from the back corner of the room where an ornate metal grate was attached to the wall, the openings between the swirly pieces of metal so narrow that it was impossible to see what lay behind it.

He looked at Will and Ellen, not knowing what to do. It was so quiet he could hear everyone breathing. He motioned with his head to the door and slowly walked over to it. Will and Ellen stayed right behind him.

Josh turned the knob. It was locked. A feeling of terror seized his heart. "We're locked in. What should we do?" he whispered.

"We need to find a way out, but whatever you do, stay away from that grate. There's something weird going on back there," whispered Ellen.

The three of them carefully walked around the room, trying to find another way out. They were directly opposite the grate when Josh discovered a window hidden behind a heavy tapestry. He tried to push it open, but it wouldn't budge.

A suspicious sound came from behind the grate. "Hurry up," pleaded Ellen.

"I can't see anything. Grab a candle," said Josh.

Will hurried over the table, tripping over the junk piled on the floor, and tried to pry the candle out of the candelabra, but wax had dripped down its sides, holding it firmly in place. A glob of hot wax dropped onto the back of his hand. He let out a little yelp and ran back to Josh and Ellen, trying not to cry as he peeled it off. "The candle's stuck," he whimpered.

"Then it's time for Plan B." Josh reached under his clothing, into his T-shirt pocket, and pulled out a crumpled package of matches coated in dog biscuit crumbs.

Will stared at him, wide-eyed. "Those are the matches I had at home."

Josh gave him a sheepish smile. "Imagine that." The first match he struck burst into flame. He leaned over, using the flame to help him find the window catch, but in the process the match accidentally touched the bottom of the tapestry. It immediately began to smolder. Acrid black smoke filled the air, floating up to the ceiling, and flames began to lick up the sides of the wall hanging at an alarming speed.

"What do we do now? We're going to suffocate," moaned Will. Ellen began to cry.

"We have to break the door down." Josh ran toward it at full speed, throwing all his weight against it. Nothing happened.

Will grabbed the doorknob and shook it. It wouldn't budge.

By now the top half of the room was completely filled with smoke.

Ellen banged on the door with her fists. "Help! We're trapped! Let us out!"

The doorknob moved a quarter turn to the left. Josh grabbed it and kept turning. He pulled the door open just in time to see a figure in a dark cloak run down the hallway. They surged out of the room after the person, but had to flatten themselves against the wall when a group of guards rushed past them, carrying buckets of water.

"Whew. At least we're safe. That was a close one," sighed Josh.

After several wrong turns, they finally found the stairwell and made their way back to the main door. They were about to rejoin Uncle Pepik and Ben when two of the emperor's guards came running down the hall after them.

"Stop! You are under arrest by the order of the Emperor of Bohemia!" shouted one of them.

Ellen stopped in her tracks and raised her hands in surrender. Josh sprinted out the door, ran over to Uncle Pepik, and hid behind him. Will ran past Josh and continued down the cobblestone street until one of the guards grabbed him by the back of his shirt and stopped him.

Another guard ran over to Josh and tried to grab him from behind Uncle Pepik, but Josh lurched the other way so he was out of his reach.

"What is the meaning of this?" asked Pepik, looking completely confused.

The guard lunged one more time, this time catching Josh by the arm.

"Could someone please tell me what is going on?" pleaded Pepik.

"I didn't mean to make trouble, honest. They locked us in this weird room with all sorts of strange doohickeys. Everything was fine until we heard a noise from behind the grate. It was really creepy. We just had to get out," gasped Josh.

"It sounds like the emperor is up to his usual tricks." Pepik gave the guard a pointed look. "Was His Majesty spying on his visitors again?"

"Perhaps," replied the guard.

"Then the boy's actions are hardly grounds for arrest."

"The boy was seen setting fire to one of His Majesty's precious tapestries."

"What?" exclaimed Pepik. "Are you sure?"

"If you don't believe me, there's your proof." The guard pointed toward the roof. A chair had been smashed through one of the upper windows. Smoke billowed out the jagged opening.

Uncle Pepik's face sank. "Oh, Joshua," he murmured, "what have you done now?"

The other guard returned with Will and shackled him to his brother and sister.

"What are you doing?" protested Josh.

"You are convicted of destroying the emperor's property and sentenced to life imprisonment."

"What?" gasped Will. He began to sway back and forth.

Josh looked at his sister. "How can we be imprisoned? We haven't had a trial."

"This isn't Canada," said Ellen.

"Oh, I forgot."

Pepik reached over and grabbed Josh's guard by the arm. "Please, sir, take me to your commander. This is all an incredible misunderstanding. I'm sure I can convince him the boy meant no harm. He and his brother and sister don't belong in Daliborka. They won't survive the night."

Josh looked over to Ben. "What's Daliborka?"

"The tower at the end of our lane where they imprison people. Years ago, a knight named Dalibor was jailed there. He was afraid he'd go mad because he couldn't see the sky, so his friends brought him a violin. People from all over Prague stood outside the tower and listened to his beautiful music."

"Is he still there?"

"No, he was executed eight years ago."

Tears poured down Josh's cheeks. "If I find his violin and play it, will you come rescue me?" he sobbed.

Ben looked him square in the eye. "My uncle and I will get you out; I promise. It might take a while, but we won't give up until we're all together again."

The guards ignored Pepik's pleas and quietly led the children to Daliborka. The streets were dark and deserted and the night air cool, but the kids were so upset that they didn't notice their surroundings. Will dragged his feet, walking as slow as possible, trying to delay their arrival at the prison. The guards didn't seem to mind as long as he kept moving in the right direction.

Eventually they reached the tower. It was a tall, plain structure, built as part of the outer castle wall at the end of Golden Lane. Its most interesting feature was its conical red roof that was visible for miles around.

They led the children down a steep stone staircase into an empty room. One of the guards grabbed a coil of rope lying on the floor. The other guard directed them to the round hatch in the middle of the floor. He bent down and removed its metal covering.

"We can make this simple or difficult. Which will it be?" asked the guard with the rope.

"What do you mean?" asked Josh, his voice quaking.

"You're going down there," said the guard, pointing to the hatch. "It's the emperor's orders—that way there's no chance you'll escape."

"I'm going down there?" Josh leaned over and peered into the hole. It was pitch black inside.

"I can't go d– d– down there," moaned Will. He let out a high-pitched wail, his eyes rolled back in his head, and he fell backwards, landing on the floor with a thud.

"Now, I'll ask you one more time: simple or difficult?" asked Josh's guard.

Josh grimaced. "What's simple?"

"You grab the rope and we'll lower you down nicely."

Josh gulped. "And difficult?"

The guard gave him an evil smile. "If you choose not to cooperate, we'll tie you up and lower you in. If the rope slips . . ." He shrugged. "I suggest you choose the simple method."

"Okay," agreed Josh. "What about my brother?"

"I think he's made his decision," snickered the other guard. They bent down and began to tie Will up.

Ellen moved closer to Josh. He reached under his shirt, pulled out a pack of matches, and secretly passed them to her behind his back. She gave him a puzzled look.

"On the count of three," he murmured. "One."

The guards continued wrapping the rope around Will's chest. Josh secretly took the Kleenex full of gunpowder out of his waistband.

"Two."

He threw the powder over his shoulder. It spread in a thin layer on the floor behind him. Just then, Will came to and began squawking at the guards, demanding that they untie him immediately.

"Three."

Ellen struck one of the matches and tossed it behind her. The powder ignited, and the resulting flash caught everyone by surprise. The guards jumped up, alarmed, as smoke filled the air. When they started coughing, Josh saw his chance. He and Ellen sprinted across the room, grabbing Will along the way, and half dragged, half carried him up the stone steps out to Golden Lane.

They fumbled with Will's rope as they ran down the street. The last knot released and the rope fell to the ground as they passed the burned-out shell of Pepik's old laboratory.

Josh burst through the door of Pepik's new home, with Ellen and Will right behind, and slammed it shut. Uncle Pepik looked up from the letter he was writing. "You're back! I was just writing a note to the emperor requesting your release. What happened?"

"We escaped. We lit some of that gunpowder I made," said Josh.

"Gunpowder? What are you talking about?"

"You know, that stuff you threw into the fire."

Uncle Pepik rubbed the top of his head. "Oh," he said, looking completely confused. He sat there, running his hand from one ear to the other, scratching his scalp on the way across.

"Uncle Pepik, what are we going to do about this?" demanded Ben.

"Just a minute. I'm thinking."

"Do you think you could speed it up?" muttered Will.

Josh shot him a dirty look.

The sound of running footsteps echoed down the street.

"The emperor's guards are looking for you. They'll be here any minute. Ben, take them and hide. I'll try to get an audience with Rudolph's commander and clear this up," said Pepik.

"You want me to hide with them?"

"Take them to the Jewish Quarter. With all the trouble of late, that's the last place they'll look."

"But Uncle, that's on the other side of the city, across the river."

"I know, but it's the only chance they've got. If the guards find them before I settle this, they'll be on the execution block by morning."

Ben peeked out the doorway. There was no sign of the guards, so they hurried out. He led them down back alleys and secluded pathways. They ducked behind statues and trees and hid behind buildings, eventually leaving the castle grounds through a rarely used doorway. Josh felt a surge of hope as they skirted the edge of the Little Quarter and ran across the Charles Bridge, slowing down to dodge the occasional horse-drawn carriage as they crossed the Vltava River.

Josh didn't dare look around for fear he would lose Ben. As it was, he had to keep an eye on Will, who was beginning to lag behind. When they finally entered the Jewish Quarter, Ben came to an abrupt halt.

"How are you doing?" he asked.

Will bent over, gasping for breath. "I feel like I just ran a marathon. Are you trying to kill me?"

"That was hardly a marathon. You weren't anywhere near a decent racing speed."

"That was my top speed. I can't go any faster."

"Good thing you're not trying out for any sports teams," muttered Josh.

They walked down a deserted street. Rundown hovels and squalid shacks mingled with newer buildings, all cloaked in the smell of decay. Ben led them along the side of a smaller building until they reached the labyrinth of dark, narrow alleyways that ran parallel to the street. As they moved along, Josh could hear the sounds of the flocks of doves and geese that lived in their owners' homes. The combination of buildings, people, and animals didn't seem to go together.

When they passed a particularly smelly building, Josh plugged his nose. "Why does it smell so bad?"

"That's a butcher's shop. It's probably the offal you smell. My uncle buys all our meat there. He told me that every Saturday night the butcher and his wife weigh themselves and hand out their combined weight in meat to the poor."

"I sure hope they're not fat," said Will.

"What do we do now? Where are we supposed to go? It's deserted; everyone must still be in bed," observed Ellen.

"That depends on how safe you want to be. I think we should stay here until morning. If we go back too soon, before my uncle has a chance to fix things, we'll have to leave all over again, and there's no guarantee we won't get caught."

"I vote for being safe," said Ellen.

"Me, too," added Will.

Ben led them over to a wall about Josh's height. "Pull yourself over, but be quick about it. If one of the rabbis sees us here at this time of night, I'll have a lot of explaining to do. We can stay here for the night."

He hoisted himself up. A second later he was over the wall.

"Great, just what I need, wall climbing again. I thought we'd left that behind in the jungle," grumbled Will.

"Quit complaining. You didn't even try it there—you were too busy fainting," sneered Josh.

"It's not my fault I faint. I can't help it."

"Then whose fault is it?"

"I don't know. It's just one of those things that happens."

"Funny how those things always happen to you."

"Guys, guys, that's enough," scolded Ellen. "Hurry up, or we'll lose Ben. Will, you go first. Josh and I will follow."

"Yes, Mother," replied Josh. When she wasn't looking, he stuck his tongue out at her.

It was quite an effort for Will to climb over the wall. He wasn't strong enough to lift his own weight, and his knees scraped against the stones as he struggled to hoist himself up. Eventually Josh and Ellen gave him a boost and he scrambled over.

He had barely landed on the ground when Josh heard his panic-stricken voice. "This is a bad, bad idea. There's no way I'm spending the night here."

Josh looked at his sister. "What's going on?"

"I don't know."

"Josh, Ellen, stay there! Ben thinks we're going to sleep in a cemetery," shouted Will.

"Be quiet, or the entire neighborhood is going to hear you," shushed Ellen.

Josh grinned from ear to ear. "I think it's a great idea. They'll never look for us in here. Hang on—I'm coming!"

— SIX —

DRASTIC MEASURES

CRGROSSCRGROSSCRGROSSCRGROSS

Josh propelled his body over the wall and landed in the cemetery. Hundreds of gravestones covered in Hebrew characters were arranged in rows throughout the lush, park-like space. Many of the stones had sunk partly into the ground. Others were tipped at awkward angles. As he meandered around, he had to watch his steps carefully because the ground was so uneven.

"This cemetery was started over one hundred years ago. It's been full a long time, but this is all the space they were given, so they had to start burying people one on top of the other." Ben brushed away a spider web that was strung between two gravestones. "If you look at the stones, they often tell you something about the person buried there." He pointed to one with two hands arranged side by side. "That means a rabbi was buried here. See that one?" He pointed to a pair of scissors. "That person was a tailor."

"Look, a book! Maybe that person was a writer," said Ellen.

"Actually, that stands for a printer. I've seen tweezers for a doctor, a mortar and pestle for an apothecary, and a lute for an instrument maker."

"Then how do you explain this?" asked Josh, pointing to a rose on one of the gravestones.

"Her name was 'Rose,'" said Ben, grinning.

"Oh. I thought maybe she sold flowers."

"What's with the piles of stones everywhere? Don't they ever clean this place up?" asked Will.

"People leave pebbles on the graves as a sign of respect," said Ben.

Josh walked over to a particularly ornate headstone. "Then this guy must have been really important. He's got a huge stone, and look at all those pebbles."

"That's Rabbi Loew's grave. When he died last year, there was a lot of wailing. It carried on for days."

"Why?"

"He's a legend around here, you know, for the *Golem*."

"The what?"

"You've never heard of Rabbi Loew's Golem?"

Josh shook his head.

"The rabbi made a giant man out of clay."

"Big deal. We could do that, too," said Will.

Ben shook his head, barely able to hide his irritation. "I bet you couldn't bring one to life."

"How'd he do that?" asked Josh.

"He made a giant man out of clay, chanted some spells from the Cabala, engraved the word *emet*—that means truth—on his forehead, and the giant came to life."

Josh's eyes lit up. "Wow. Can you get me a book of those spells?"

"No way. The Golem was made for a specific purpose. His job was to stop the people who were spreading lies about the Jews and persecuting them. Trust me, you wouldn't want to mess with the Golem."

"Where is he now?" asked Ellen.

"Eventually the emperor promised to protect the Jews, so Rabbi Loew took the Golem aside and told him they didn't need his help anymore. The Golem didn't like that, so the rabbi quickly erased the first letter from his forehead, changing *emet* to *met*, which means death, and the Golem died. That night, the rabbi and his helpers hauled the Golem's clay into the attic of the synagogue and covered it with old prayer books. They say it's still there."

"Can we go see it? Please, please, please?" begged Josh.

"We're not breaking into the synagogue. That would be a terrible thing to do," said Ben.

"Come on. We wouldn't hurt anything. I just want to take a look."

Will cleared his throat. "Remember what happened the last time you said that?"

"Ben's right. The reason we're in this cemetery is because you used a match to 'take a look,' and look what that got us. Trouble . . . big trouble," said Ellen.

"I'm with Ellen. We're done exploring for today. What do we do now?" asked Will.

"Find a comfortable spot for the night. We'll head back in the morning," said Ben.

"But I don't want to sleep here," said Will.

"Too bad," said Josh. He didn't feel one bit sorry for his brother.

Will sat down, his back to the wall, muttering away as he tried not to notice the way the breeze moved the leaves of the elder trees that shaded the cemetery, or the long, dark shadows the moon created behind each gravestone.

Ellen sat down with Ben, chatting happily.

Josh lay down on the grass on top of one of the higher graves, closed his eyes, and fell asleep.

The sun wasn't quite up when Will woke everyone up.

Josh rolled onto his side. "Where am I?" he muttered. He opened his eyes a crack. "Oh, that's right, the cemetery."

Will nudged him again.

"Leave me alone. I'm still sleeping."

"We need to get out of here. I'm exhausted. I spent the whole night standing guard, just in case the Golem came back to life and decided to get us."

"That's nice," mumbled Josh.

Frustrated by his brother's response, Will walked over to Ellen and Ben, who were already awake.

"Can we go back to Uncle Pepik's now?" asked Ellen.

"We can try. We'll walk to the lane together. You can hide while I see my uncle and make sure everything's okay. If it is, I'll come get you." Ben let out a big yawn. "I'm with Josh. I didn't get enough sleep, either. It's going to be a long day."

The walk back to Golden Lane was uneventful. The streets were quiet, except for the crowing of roosters. Josh pranced over the Charles Bridge, swinging his arms back and forth as though he didn't have a care in the world, while the others trudged along behind.

They sneaked into the castle grounds through Daliborka. The tower was completely empty, so they stopped for a minute to survey the damage done by Josh's gunpowder. The room was intact, but the walls were covered in a layer of black soot.

"Good thing I didn't have more gunpowder, or I'd have blown the place up," said Josh.

"And killed all of us in the process," complained Will.

"Come on, we have to keep moving. We had better be quiet. Most of the alchemists will have been up all night tending their furnaces. I don't want any of them to see us," said Ben.

"Why not?" asked Josh.

"I don't trust the people around here. Everyone is out for themselves. They'll squeal on you in a heartbeat if they think it will keep them on the emperor's good side. We can't afford to take any chances."

They left the tower and walked down Golden Lane. Ben stopped. "Wait over there," he said, pointing to a narrow alleyway. "I'll come get you if everything's all right."

Will wrapped his arms around his chest. "What if you don't come back?"

"Then you're on your own." He slipped away before Will could question him further.

The three of them trudged down the narrow alleyway between the two buildings. Josh looked back over his shoulder. Six of the emperor's guards marched down the lane after Ben. "Oh, no," he exclaimed.

"What?" said Will.

"I just saw six guards go after Ben. I think he's in trouble."

"This is your fault. I'm holding you responsible."

"What do you mean? How can you blame me for this?"

"Number one: You touched the stone after I specifically asked you not to. There might have been a better place for us to go, but you didn't even give us a chance to find out.

Number two: You set Rudolph's tapestry on fire. If you hadn't been so stupid and lit that match, we wouldn't have been sent to Daliborka to be executed."

Will's voice grew frantic as he continued. "Number three: If we hadn't gone to Daliborka, you wouldn't have lit that gunpowder, and we wouldn't have been forced to run away and spend the night in the cemetery, and I would have gotten some sleep. I'm going to have a lousy day, and it's all your fault!"

Josh could feel his temper bubbling up inside of him. He looked around for something to throw, but the only thing in the alleyway was a tiny gray kitten that mewed as it rubbed against Ellen's leg. He glared at his brother for a long minute, and then, just when Will thought everything was going to be okay, Josh wound up and punched him as hard as he could, right in the stomach.

Will bent over, moaning and gasping for air. Ellen rushed to his side to help, but he pushed her away.

"What did you do that for?" asked Ellen, her voice rising. She wiped a tear from her eye. "If Dad were here, he'd ground you for a month, and you know it."

"I'm tired of being picked on all the time. He thinks everything is my fault." Josh's eyes filled with tears. "It's not my fault he's such a wimp. He should learn how to handle things better. I've been doing the best I can. I didn't mean to make so much trouble." He raised his voice and yelled, "And just so you know, I'm tired and hungry, too!"

"I don't care. That's no excuse."

"Fine. Side with him if you want. From now on, I'm on my own." He stalked down the alleyway and turned the corner toward Uncle Pepik's house.

"Ah, Joshua, there you are, and just in time. I need someone to load up the athanor with charcoal. I must say, I prefer charcoal as opposed to that ancient wood-burning furnace I had in my other laboratory," said Uncle Pepik.

"Is it safe for me to be here? Aren't the guards after us?"

"All is well. After several hours of exasperating conversation with the commander, he agreed that the whole situation was a big misunderstanding and decided to set you free. There is one provision, however. I had to promise that I would keep you under my wing and ensure that you didn't get into any more trouble, so no more fires or explosions. You must be on your best behavior, or the commander assured me you'd be left to die in Daliborka."

Josh plopped down on a nearby chair and sat there, hunched over. "I guess that's all right, but it'll cramp my style," he mumbled.

"What was that, son?"

"Oh, nothing. How much charcoal should I put in the fire?"

"More than you put into that black powder you made," replied Uncle Pepik, chuckling. "I still can't believe you blew up my laboratory. My goodness, what a surprise. I now understand what Sir Roger Bacon meant in his Latin anagram of 1242. He was describing how to make the exact mixture you created. I read his instructions many times and never quite grasped them, but now I do. Your little experiment greatly enlightened me. Thank you."

"Um, you're welcome, I think. Where's Ben?"

"He went to get your brother and sister. They'll be back shortly."

"Too bad," muttered Josh, carefully pouring a shovel full of charcoal into Pepik's athanor.

When Ben returned with Will and Ellen, they joined Josh in assisting Pepik. Ellen and Will washed the glass alembics and earthenware containers and arranged them in rows above the workbench, taking care to avoid their brother as much as possible. Josh kept the furnace stoked with charcoal, regularly opening and closing the vents so the temperature remained constant. Uncle Pepik carefully measured different powders, liquids, and dried plants, which he placed in the cucurbit, the lower part of the container that held the materials being distilled. Josh helped him fit the alembic on top, with its long, narrow spout for the condensation to pour out, and they sealed the two pieces together with lute, a sticky mixture made of dung and egg whites.

They were about to break for lunch—scrambled egg yolks, stale bread, and a lump of disgusting cheese—when Scottie and his dogs poked their heads through the door.

"Well, well, Old Pepik, you certainly are full of surprises. Here you are, in a brand new lab that you do not deserve, working with not one, but four assistants. How nice," he snickered.

Pepik looked up from his work. "I'm sorry, but I can't spare the time to visit. I'm at a critical stage in my work. Is there something I can do for you?"

"When I appeared in the emperor's court this morning I was dismayed to learn that you had been granted permission to work with four assistants, when so many of us on Golden Lane have none. When I brought this to the commander's attention, he immediately agreed that an injustice had been done."

Pepik didn't bother to look up from his work. "And your point?"

"In order to rectify this situation, the emperor has proclaimed that there will be a contest tomorrow morning. The first alchemist to produce the philosopher's stone will be awarded these four young people as apprentices, as well as more apparatus, supplies, and a personal servant to cook and clean for them. I suggest you be prepared, old man, because I, Edward Geronimo Scotta, expect to be the victor."

Scottie stared at Pepik, holding his breath as he waited for his reply. Pepik looked at him, closed his eyes, and stood there, gently swaying back and forth.

Scottie finally gave up, turned on his heel, and stomped off, with Apollo and Zeus ambling along behind.

Ben rushed over to his uncle. "Uncle Pepik, what's the matter? Are you okay?"

Uncle Pepik held up his hand. "Just a minute, lad," he murmured.

The children stood there, waiting for him to snap out of whatever was happening to him. After several minutes, which seemed more like hours, Pepik opened his eyes. "Thank you. I was praying."

"Oh," said Ben, letting out a sigh of relief. "You scared me. I thought something bad was happening."

"My goodness, no. I'm fine but very concerned. I cannot move the experiment at this critical time, and there is much work to be done before I can demonstrate my work to anyone, much less the emperor. On the other hand, I do not want the four of you to end up with one of the charlatans on the lane, especially someone like Scottie. He would not treat you well. I guess we don't have a choice. We must get to work. There is much to do before the elixir will be ready."

He walked over to his cot, knelt down, and lifted up one of the floorboards. A small rectangular cavity lay beneath it, filled with the three books that had been spared from the fire in his other cottage. He pulled two of them out, repositioned the board, and carried them over to the table.

"I've never seen those books before, Uncle. What are you reading?" asked Ben.

"Drastic times call for drastic measures. I was going to review these instructions when I was further along, but there is no time." He paged through one of the books until he found the spot he was looking for.

"Ah, here it is. I've always appreciated the work of Bernard of Treves but found his concepts difficult to apply. Perhaps today will be better."

By the time night fell, Pepik and his crew had squeezed a week's worth of work into one day. After a small supper of soup with liver dumplings—which Ellen refused to eat—and sour green apples that Uncle Pepik had picked from a nearby tree long before they were ripe, the children collapsed on the floor, exhausted, and quickly fell asleep.

Pepik was pacing back and forth, talking to himself, when Josh woke up. "Uncle Pepik, I have to go to the bathroom," he whispered.

"Go outside. Take care not to wake the others," he whispered back.

Golden Lane was completely still. Josh shivered as he ran down the street toward the back alley. He stopped when he noticed a light burning in Scottie's laboratory.

He walked over to the window and peeked inside. Scottie was standing in the middle of the room, dressed in a long flowing cape, glaring at his furnace where a glass alembic gently bubbled away. The dogs were lying at his feet. Apollo was resting her chin on his foot. Every time he moved, she moved with him. Zeus was snoring so loudly that it sounded like a train was passing through the cottage.

The room was a mess. A grimy jumble of instruments, manuscripts, and several skulls overflowed onto Scottie's workbench. A tattered chair was perched beside his furnace, its stuffing oozing out of the holes in the seat and arms. Heaps of dirty clothes and broken equipment covered most of the floor.

As Josh watched, Scottie grabbed the alembic and hurled it at the floor. Shards of glass flew everywhere, and the murky liquid splattered the entire room. Josh gasped. "That's just like the picture on our wall." Zeus woke up, and the two dogs bolted to the other side of the room. Scottie leaned back and howled, scaring Josh so badly that he ran back to Uncle Pepik's without going to the bathroom.

He jerked the door open and rushed in, ready to tell Uncle Pepik

what he had seen, but the old man was quietly sitting in his chair, praying. Not wanting to interrupt, Josh took his place on the floor. He lay
there for a long time, wondering if either alchemist would succeed and
what turn of events the morning would bring.

SEVEN

THE PRESENTATION

M orning arrived too soon. At the appointed time, Pepik gathered up all his materials—glass containers filled with various liquids, earthenware vessels containing dried herbs and plants, two books, and willow baskets of firewood and charcoal—and carried the first load to the emperor's laboratory, while the children continued packing.

They were almost finished when Pepik reappeared in the doorway, looking completely perturbed. "What's the matter, Uncle?" asked Ben.

"Something is not right. I know I'm forgetting something." He ran his hand over his head. "Well, whatever it is, we'll have to work without it." He picked up a crate, led the children out, and closed the door behind them.

They hadn't walked far when Scottie flew by, a book in one hand, and Apollo and Zeus's leashes in the other. "Hello!" he cried as the dogs dragged him down the lane. Before Pepik could return the greeting Scottie was around the corner, out of sight.

"Remind me never to get an English mastiff," said Will.

"They are quite a bit of work, but I imagine he enjoys the attention they bring," replied Pepik.

They reached the end of Golden Lane and walked into another courtyard. A nervous feeling fluttered through Josh's stomach. "Uncle Pepik, where are we going?"

"To Powder Tower. His Majesty has a special laboratory there. I understand it's been vacant the past month. The last charlatan was kicked out after they discovered he produced fool's gold, not the real thing."

"How did he do that?"

"He slipped some into his crucible when no one was looking."

They continued on past the majestic cathedral and through the palace to Powder Tower. The tower was a recent addition, built fourteen years earlier to house the cannons that overlooked Stag Moat. Pepik led them up a steep stone staircase. By the third flight, Josh's legs ached so badly he thought they were going to fall off. He breathed a sigh of relief when they finally walked through an arched opening into a large round room.

The emperor's laboratory was bright and cheerful, a marked contrast to the dreary cottages on Golden Lane. It had newly plastered walls, a freshly swept floor partially covered by a large Turkish rug, blue velvet curtains on the tall windows, and a vaulted ceiling.

The laboratory was stocked with the newest, finest equipment money could buy. Crates of gleaming glassware were stacked on the floor, the glass wrapped in straw to protect it from breakage. Two large brick hearths had been built along the outer walls between the windows. Four freestanding athanors, metal crucibles, shelves of alchemical texts, and baskets of charcoal rounded out the room.

Josh and Ben were standing on one side of a workbench and Will and Ellen on the other helping Uncle Pepik unpack his supplies, when Apollo and Zeus surged into the room, panting heavily. Scottie breezed in behind them, dressed in his best robe and a long cloak lined with purple satin.

"Well, well, what do we have here? The old alchemist from down the lane who's never had any success of consequence, and his four apprentices who will soon be joining me. This shall be an interesting day, old man. Good luck. You're going to need it."

"What's with the 'old' stuff? Scottie looks as old as your uncle," whispered Josh.

"He's just trying to throw us off. Don't worry, everything will be fine," said Ben.

"How about we split up the children now? We can each have two for the day. It would only be fair," suggested Scottie.

Josh moved closer to Uncle Pepik. Pepik sighed. "The children stay with me until the emperor says otherwise. Now, please, let me work in peace. There is much to do and so little time."

"Fine," snarled Scottie. "You'll regret your decision. I was planning to return your nephew to you after I won, but I've changed my mind. Too bad." He spun around and stalked out the door, his cloak flapping behind him. Apollo and Zeus bounded after him, their leashes dragging on the floor.

"Children, ignore him if you can. I suspect he will be difficult all day. We need to stay focused on the task at hand. Ellen, please crush the leaves in the brown earthenware container. Ben, light a fire. I think I would prefer that athanor," he said, pointing to one of the furnaces, "but don't make it too hot. We need to build up the heat slowly."

"Yes, Uncle," replied Ben.

"And boys, you can set up the alembics. I have three different ones I would like to work with today: one main one and two backups. Once you've mixed the lute, I'll show you how I'd like everything arranged. Can you manage that?"

"We'll try," said Josh.

Pepik breathed a sigh of relief. "Thank you. Come now, we must hurry. Let's get to work."

Scottie reappeared twenty minutes later, carrying a large wooden crate. A group of the emperor's guards entered the room after him, followed by a few curious bystanders. The guards took their places around the alchemists, watching intently for anything out of the ordinary.

Apollo and Zeus lay down in the middle of the floor, their eyes never leaving their master. Scottie lit a coal on one of the hearths, set his crucible on top of it, and stacked a pile of books on a nearby table. He opened the top book, propped it up, and pulled up a comfortable looking chair. Taking a step back, he examined the arrangement and then fiddled with it until he was satisfied. His work done, he dropped something into his crucible and sat down to wait, chatting away with the emperor's men as he watched Pepik.

Pepik sat hunched over his alembic, his brow furrowed as he monitored the heat in the furnace with deep concentration. "Ben, come here! I need help managing the rotational fire. I can't seem to keep it steady."

Ben rushed over with a bellows and blew a stream of air across the coals. Within seconds they turned bright orange. "Ah, that's better. Thank you, son. There are days I wish I could master the dry method, but every attempt I've made has been disastrous. Using the alembic is such a complicated process."

"How is it coming, Uncle?"

"I've purified this solution enough," he said, motioning to the murky gray liquid in the cucurbit. "If it's going to do something, today would be as good a day as any."

Just then, the commander entered the room. He was short yet powerfully built, with a square jaw and closely cropped hair. His beady eyes scanned the room, taking in the dueling alchemists, Pepik's four apprentices, the emperor's guards, and the others who were there to witness the presentations.

"Well, well, if it isn't His Majesty's beloved commander. And how are things with you this fine day?" asked Scottie.

The commander ignored his question. "Are you ready?"

"My, no time to chitchat, I see." Scottie stood up, picked up a small earthenware container from his table, and carefully poured two drops of reddish brown liquid into his crucible. "Almost ready, Commander. I shall not be long. Where are the other contestants?"

"They're coming later. We'll start with you two."

"Oh," muttered Scottie.

"What about you?" barked the commander in Pepik's direction.

Pepik was so completely enthralled with the changes taking place in his alembic that he didn't hear him.

"I asked you a question, Zelenka. Are you ready?"

Ben tugged on his sleeve. "Uncle Pepik, the commander is speaking to you."

"What?" mumbled Pepik. When he looked up, he realized the commander was staring at him. "Something's happening. This might be it," he twittered.

Everyone rushed over. Josh pushed his way to the front and watched, his heart pounding, as a spectacular transformation took place in the glass vessel. The murky liquid that Pepik had been distilling had turned from gray to black.

"The 'Crow's Head,'" gasped Scottie. "I've read about it."

They continued watching as a white halo appeared around the edge of the liquid, and thin white threads shot toward the center, like rays of light. Soon the entire solution was pure white.

Uncle Pepik fell to his knees. "Please, dear Lord, let this be the day. May today be the day I see the glory of your original creation in this vessel."

"We need to test this. If this truly is the white elixir, it will turn base metal to silver," said the commander.

"No! We can't test it now. If it is the white elixir, I'm only a few steps away from the red elixir. Just let me continue a little while longer."

The commander frowned. "The emperor gave me strict instructions to bring news of any success, no matter how small, to his attention. He will want this information immediately."

"Just a few more minutes, please?"

"Don't make me regret this."

Pepik leaned over toward Josh and Ben. "I'm going to run back to the cottage and get some additional equipment. Maybe it will speed things up. Don't let Scottie touch anything," he whispered. The boys nodded in agreement.

Pepik approached the commander and quietly asked his permission to leave. When Josh turned to see what else was happening, he noticed one of Rudolph's guards slip quietly out of the room.

Ben was busy manning the bellows, and Uncle Pepik was still trying to convince the commander that he needed to return to his cottage when Josh heard a faint cracking noise. He leaned over the alembic and discovered a hairline crack working its way up the side of the vessel. "Um, Uncle Pepik, come here, quick."

Pepik turned away from the commander. "What is it?"

"There's a crack in the glass—a big one."

"What?" Pepik ran over to his equipment. "No, this can't be happening, not now when I've finally created the white elixir." A fleeting look of desperation crossed his face. "Everyone, move back. Ben, stop the bellows, now!"

Everyone slowly walked backwards, through the doorway to the landing. Pepik inspected his equipment once more. "No, please don't let this happen. Not now, when I'm so close. Please, dear Lord, have mercy on me."

He stood there, watching and waiting. The guards started getting restless.

"Come on, old man, let us back in. You're a failure," taunted Scottie.

"Please, just one more minute. If it cools slowly enough, it might be okay."

A loud crack was his reply. It reverberated across the room and the entire alembic exploded, sending bits of glass and drops of elixir everywhere.

Pepik fell to his knees, sobbing. "No, this can't be happening. Not when I was so close."

"What did I tell you? You're a failure, old man, a fool and a failure. You'll never succeed," jeered Scottie.

The commander walked over to Pepik and helped him to his feet. "I hope you can match those cruel words with some results of your own, Scotta. Show me something, now," he growled.

Scottie ran over to his crucible. He picked up his wand, plunged it into the molten metal, and gave it a stir. The commander peered into his container. "So?"

"Just a minute. It needs a bit more stirring."

Josh moved closer. He noticed Scottie was shaking and his brow was covered in sweat.

"I'm waiting," said the commander.

Scottie peered into his crucible again. "It's almost ready. Just one more minute." He gave the solution a few more stirs. "Well, well, what do we have here? Imagine, a crucible full of pure silver, and I didn't even need the white elixir to create it." He gave the group a smug grin.

"What?" said Pepik. He and the children ran over and looked in. A lump of silver about the size of a marble lay in the bottom of Scottie's crucible. "I don't believe it. How did you do that?"

"When you start with the purest of mercury, the process is sped up enormously. I worked at length on my preparations last night."

Pepik hung his head, unable to believe what had just taken place. "I guess you win. Please take good care of the children. They are wonderful and have been an enormous help to me."

Josh grabbed Pepik by the shoulder and stood on his tiptoes so he could whisper into his ear. "Last night when I went out to go to the bathroom, I saw Scottie throw his alembic onto the floor. It made a huge mess, and then he let out a terrible howl. I don't think he made anything last night. It looked to me like something went wrong."

Pepik pulled away and pondered this information for a moment. He looked Josh square in the eye. "Are you certain, lad? This isn't time to be making up stories just to save your hide."

"It's the truth, honest."

"All right, then." Pepik turned to the commander. "Before I concede, I have one request."

"And what might that be?"

"I believe it would be prudent to thoroughly inspect Scottie's equipment, just to make sure no trickery was involved."

All the blood drained from Scottie's face. He stared at Josh, his eyes full of hate.

A shiver ran up Josh's spine. He felt like running out of the room as fast as he could, but he willed his feet to stay anchored to the floor.

The commander slowly nodded. "Yes, that is an excellent suggestion. Guards, examine his equipment."

— EIGHT —

THE PROCLAMATION

The guards took Scottie's equipment apart, piece by piece. Everything appeared to be in order until they reached his wand. The commander carried it over to the window, held it up to one eye, and peered down its shaft.

"Scotta, I'm disappointed in you. I thought you would have learned by now."

Scottie snorted. "You and I both know the stone can't be made. The emperor appears to be the only one who hasn't figured that out. I'm hardly unique in this bit of deception. Everyone uses trickery."

"No, Scottie, the use of trickery is never appropriate. Guards, take him to Daliborka."

The guards led him out of the room. He went along peacefully, chatting to them as if they were old friends. Apollo and Zeus trotted along behind.

"What was that all about?" asked Will.

"Scottie used an old trick, the hollow wand," explained Ben. "When he plunged his wand into the hot liquid, it melted the wax on the end, allowing the silver hidden inside to fall out."

"I pity that poor fellow. He should know better. I guess he felt he had to produce something today or risk losing the emperor's patronage," said Pepik. He absentmindedly wandered over to his equipment and began to clean up. The children joined him, gathering his alembics, sweeping up the shards of glass, and wiping spatters of elixir. The disappointment of the lost experiment was tempered by their relief that they wouldn't have to work for Scottie. They worked silently for a while, lost in their own thoughts.

"It's strange that the emperor wasn't here. You'd think he'd want to see this," mused Ellen.

"I'm not surprised. I think it's just another sign of his insanity. They say he sits for hours at his zoo, staring at his beloved lion," replied Ben, glancing both ways to see if any guards were around.

"He has his own zoo?" exclaimed Josh. "Boy, I'd sure like to be an emperor."

"His royal garden runs behind the castle. I've never seen it—it's off limits to everyone but his inner circle—but I've heard it's beautiful. There are long hedges of tulips in the spring, an orangery and greenhouses, and lots of statues and fountains."

"We have parks like that where we live, too. What's the big deal?" asked Will.

"Many of his animals run wild in the moat that runs through it; he has bears, leopards, panthers, and a bunch of exotic birds. And of course, everyone knows about his African lion."

Josh raised his eyebrows.

"You haven't heard about his African lion?"

"No."

"Last year, one of the emperor's astrologers predicted that his pet lion will die right before he does."

"That's creepy. If I were him, I wouldn't want to know that."

"They say that ever since, the lion has received better care than the emperor himself."

"I guess that makes sense in a weird kind of way."

The boys walked over to Uncle Pepik and the commander, who were deep in conversation.

"Zelenka, I am impressed. You made great progress today, more than I've seen from anyone in years. Imagine, the white elixir. You've outdone yourself. That was truly brilliant," said the commander.

Despite his profound disappointment, a tiny smile stole onto Pepik's face. "Thank you, sir." The commander nodded and left the room, leaving Pepik and the children alone.

"You know what I've been thinking about?" said Will.

Pepik shook his head.

"Scottie's name. What were his parents thinking? You've got to admit, Edward Geronimo Scotta is a pretty bad name."

"It's probably not his real name. He may have chosen it for effect," said Pepik.

"My brother's name isn't much better. I bet you can't guess what his full name is," said Josh. Ellen gave him a warning jab in the side.

"Come on, tell us," said Ben.

"His name is William Ogilvy Hubert MacKenzie. Pretty bad, huh?"

Pepik chuckled. "What were your parents thinking?"

"I can't help it. It's Josh's fault," he whined. "Our parents didn't know they were having twins until the day we were born. My dad was so shocked when Josh was born that he fainted in the delivery room. My name was supposed to be William Joshua MacKenzie, but they needed to come up with another boy's name fast, so they gave my middle name to Josh. Now that I think about it, it was a good thing. I sure wouldn't want his name."

Josh wound up and was about to punch his brother in the stomach when Pepik grabbed him by the arm. "That's enough, boys. You fight over the most ridiculous matters."

"But Uncle Pepik, he was being rude to me. He was making fun of my name," protested Josh.

"And likewise, you to him. I want you to drop this matter at once."

He was about to say more, but was interrupted when a guard marched into the room bearing a scroll with the emperor's seal.

"Hey, that's the guy I saw sneak out of here before," said Josh, pointing at the man. "I wonder what he wants."

The guard cleared his throat several times, until he had everyone's attention. "Hear ye, hear ye, I come bearing a proclamation from His Majesty Rudolph II, Emperor of Bohemia. Upon hearing of the success in this laboratory today, and in recognition of the ongoing fraud that has plagued his court, the emperor requires that by tomorrow, every alchemist on Golden Lane must bring four drams of authentic philosopher's stone to Powder Tower for services rendered, or be forcibly removed from their premises and escorted out of Prague."

"What?" gasped Pepik. "One day is hardly enough to produce the work of a lifetime."

"Your success brought about this proclamation. When I notified the emperor about your white elixir, he was so pleased that he insisted we continue the contest tomorrow."

"In light of my work today, surely I am excluded from this proclamation."

The guard unrolled the scroll farther, scanned its length, and looked at Pepik with compassion in his eyes. "I'm sorry, sir, but there are no exclusions. His Majesty did say, however, that he was contemplating appointing you Imperial Counselor, should you succeed."

Josh jumped up and down. "Does that mean I'll have to call you Sir Pepik? Hey, maybe you can get me a suit of armor!"

Pepik looked at the commander, who had returned while the proclamation was being read. "Sir, I am not interested in receiving honors from the emperor. Surely you can speak to him on my behalf. After what you witnessed today, it is obvious that I am well along in my work."

"I will gladly speak to His Majesty on your behalf, but I am not optimistic." The commander leaned forward. "He is not known for his logic of late," he whispered. He took a step back and continued, his deep voice booming across the room. "I shall try and have a brief audience with His Majesty this afternoon and shall report back to you this evening."

Pepik grabbed him by the arm. "Thank you, my friend, thank you. I will be at my cottage should you wish to speak to me."

Josh and his siblings were back at the cottage helping Uncle Pepik unpack when Scottie poked his head through the door. Apollo and Zeus tried to slip past him, but he held them back. "Well, well, if it isn't the studious alchemist and his motley crew of helpers."

Uncle Pepik sighed and put down his alembic. "How did you manage to get out of Daliborka so quickly?"

"I wheedled my way out by sweet-talking the guards. It's amazing what people will do for a few drops of elixir that will heal their physical woes."

"Does your elixir actually do anything?"

"Maybe," he replied with a smirk.

"I was hoping you would have given up your devious ways. Will you ever quit this trickery?"

"I don't expect to in this lifetime, although if I were to ingest some of that stone you are about to create, I might embark on a life of honesty." He gave Pepik a devilish grin. "On second thought, I think not. That would be too boring."

Pepik sighed again. "Scottie, we have work to do, and so do you, I presume. You'd best be on your way."

"And that, my dear friend, is exactly why I'm here. As I see it, we are both in a bind. Each of us has to produce the philosopher's stone by tomorrow or face eviction from this street, though I must admit, I regularly long for a more sumptuous dwelling."

"I am content here in my cottage. It meets all my needs quite nicely."

Scottie decided to try another tactic. "Pepik, may I speak boldly?"

"Please do, but be quick about it. As I said before, I have much to do."

"I would like to propose that we work together. You might have created the stone if it weren't for the weakness in the glass. I have years of training and am certain that I would have much to contribute to your work over the next day."

"And what if we create it?"

"Why, isn't the answer obvious?"

"If I thought it was obvious, I wouldn't have asked the question."

"We would both possess unlimited wealth and eternal life. Would that be so bad?"

"And what of our responsibility to the emperor?" asked Pepik.

"I say that if we create the stone before tomorrow's presentation, we quietly leave this place, once and for all."

"So the emperor gets nothing, despite the fact that he has supported us for the past few years."

"Supported us? You call these hovels we live in and the antiquated equipment he lends us 'support'?"

"Yes, as a matter of fact, I do."

"Fine, then we shall leave Rudolph one dram of the stone as payment for services rendered."

"I believe we should give him all of it and let him reward us as he sees fit."

Scottie frowned. "You are far too generous, old man. Don't you desire riches?"

"To be honest, I do not. It has always been my secret desire that if the Lord chose to bless me with the gift of the stone, I would use it to make gold for his church."

Scottie gave him a condescending smile. "As I said, you are far too generous, old man."

"Of course, there is another alternative. What if we fail? Then who bears the consequences?"

"In my mind, there is no room for failure, so the answer to your question is simple. We will plant a lump of gold up your sleeve, and then, if circumstances dictate, you can drop it into the crucible at the correct time and impress the emperor."

"But that's fraud."

"No one will suspect you. You have a squeaky-clean reputation and enjoy the respect of the court and the lane alike. I would be willing to rehearse the illusion with you until your trickery is undetectable. See? The plan is foolproof. No matter what happens, we are free," he said, grinning from ear to ear. "I must say, it's positively brilliant."

"That's one way to describe it," muttered Josh.

"Scottie, I have no choice but to turn you down. I have no desire to partake in your fraudulent exploits, and I am absolutely certain that you do not possess the spiritual principles necessary to make the stone in an honest way. Your words drip with honey, but I know in my heart you would bamboozle me without a second thought if you had the chance." Pepik turned to the children. "Come now, children, we must begin."

Scottie's face grew red. "You are a fool, old man, an absolute fool. I will personally see to it that you will regret your decision as long as you live." He stomped out the door.

Uncle Pepik let out one final sigh. "My goodness, that man has nerve. Let's get to work. We must reproduce the exact conditions that led to the creation of the white elixir, and then try to distill it further from there. Are you ready, my faithful assistants?"

"Of course, Uncle. We are always ready," replied Ben.

Josh was standing next to the workbench, grinding some dried leaves with the mortar and pestle, while Pepik quickly gathered the ingredients he needed for the next distillation.

"Uncle Pepik, there's something I've been wondering about: Why do they call the philosopher's stone a 'stone' if it's not a stone? Ben said it's a liquid that people can drink," Josh said.

"That's a good question. In the writing of the ancients, they refer to the philosopher's stone as a stone, yet not a stone. It is described as the most precious thing in the world, yet the most common. Making it is difficult, yet child's play. It is found nowhere, yet at the same time, everywhere. Best of all, if it is allowed to grow, it will bring its maker eternal life and riches beyond understanding, here on earth as well as in heaven."

"I have no idea what you're talking about."

"I think what the ancients were trying to say is that making the stone is difficult, but once you understand the process and your heart is right, you will be surprised at how easy it is."

"Oh." Josh paused. "How does it give people eternal life? I thought only Jesus could do that."

"I have never drunk any myself, but I believe it slows the process of aging. Some say that it will give you an extra one hundred years on earth, while others say you will never die. I personally believe that the maximum lifespan for an alchemist is one thousand years. Based on my studies, I believe God made this limit. It is the maximum time that a person can make himself young again."

"Do you know of any people who lived that long?"

"It is said that some of the alchemists of old have reappeared from time to time in various cities, especially Paris. I haven't seen any of them myself, but I believe the people who saw them and told me about it. It is said that the adepts, alchemists who have created the stone, share their special knowledge with others who are worthy. That's why you find them popping up from time to time, dispensing their knowledge, and then quietly continuing on with their lives. Sometimes I think it would be wonderful not to grow old, to avoid watching your body slowly fail you."

"If someone offered you the elixir, would you drink it?"

"That is an excellent question. I can tell you're a real thinker."

Josh smiled. There was a long pause while Pepik pondered his question.

"So, would you?" Josh asked again.

"I don't know. Most people think living hundreds of years would be wonderful, but I'm not sure it would be such a good thing. A person might become bored or weary of life if they had to live that long. One of the reasons life is so special, so sweet, is that we know we don't have forever. Our time on earth is limited. That's why we have to use our time well."

"So you wouldn't drink the elixir?"

"As someone near the end of their earthly life, I must confess there are days I long for heaven. In many ways, my life has been a long and painful struggle, with only little spurts of joy. I long to see my Lord face to face, as well as my wife, Danica, and our son, Markus. She died forty years ago giving birth to him, and he died of the plague at age three. Even after all these years, I still miss them."

"So you want to live the rest of your life like a normal person, and then die and be with your family in heaven?"

"Yes, that is correct, dear boy. That is correct."

"Can I ask you a few more questions?"

"Sure. I'll set up the alembic while we're talking."

"Why does everyone want gold so bad? What's so great about it?"

"Gold is a symbol of many things, but especially of life and wealth, the two things most people desire. If you bury a piece of gold in the ground and leave it for a thousand years, it will be as shiny and beautiful the day you dig it up as the day you buried it. It never tarnishes. People value it so highly, however, because it allows them to buy whatever they want."

"That would be pretty awesome."

"I don't know. I am quite content with my life. True alchemists are never interested in gaining the philosopher's stone for great wealth. I believe that when we get too much of anything, it loses its charm. This can apply to an extra long life as well as unlimited riches."

Josh was quiet for a moment. "I've never thought about it that way before, but when I get tons of candy at Halloween and Easter, after a while I don't even care about it. I just eat it because I have it, not because I think it tastes that good or because I really want to."

Pepik looked up. "What is this 'Halloween' you are speaking of? Oh, never mind," he mumbled. He turned back to this work. "We shall discuss it later. Today of all days I must keep my mind focused on the Great Work."

Josh watched as Pepik carefully positioned the alembic on top of the cucurbit. "Can I ask you one more question if it's about alchemy?"

Pepik nodded.

"Why wouldn't you let Scottie work with us? Shouldn't you have given him a chance?"

"Alchemy only works if you have a reached certain maturity. If you're not ready to receive the knowledge, you won't understand it. If your heart isn't right, you won't be able to grasp its secrets. I believe this is Scottie's problem. Because he's not ready, he would rather trick people than do the hard work it takes to become the right kind of person to be an alchemist. At the best of times, our experiments are delicate and rarely repeatable, because so much depends on the alchemist and his heart.

"I am not willing to risk our success on Scottie. I know his heart is troubled, and I fear it would impact our work. No matter how hard we try, we cannot succeed without the assistance of God, and I am quite sure our Lord doesn't approve of Scottie's motives."

"I guess that makes sense. I thought maybe you were mad at him for cheating."

"I was never angry, Joshua, just disappointed. Scottie's choices give all alchemists a bad name."

"Can I ask you one more question?"

Pepik nodded.

"Do you think the stone can really turn other metals into gold?"

"Before I answer, I have some questions for you. Do you believe grains of sand can be transformed into clear glass?"

"I don't know."

Pepik smiled. "They can. That's what glass is made from. Do you believe that by human skill, we can remove minerals from the earth and turn them into ore?"

"You mean like what a blacksmith does? I met a blacksmith when we were in England."

"A blacksmith doesn't do that, but a smelter can. Do you believe that a small bit of yeast can turn water, flour, and sugar into a delicious loaf of bread?"

"I know that happens. I've watched my mom bake bread before. I love fresh bread."

"Then maybe it's possible that base metals can be transmuted into gold."

Josh stared at him, his mouth hanging open.

"Maybe unexplainable and unimaginable things occur when you add the philosopher's stone to base metal. Maybe it can transform metal into pure gold." Pepik picked up one of his ancient books. "I'll leave you to ponder that," he added before heading over to his velvet chair for further reading.

— NINE —

MIDNIGHT VISITOR

CRBOÐCACRBOÐCACRBOÐCACRBO

Night had fallen, and everyone was quietly going about their work. A quick meal of cold beetroot soup, leftover dumplings, and cabbage filled Josh's stomach but didn't satisfy his hunger. He found himself longing for something fresh and hot. Despite this, he managed to perform his tasks with a sense of duty and concentration, until a quiet knock on the door interrupted his work.

"I wonder who's calling at this late hour. I am not accustomed to receiving visitors at this time of night," said Pepik. He walked over to the door and opened it. The commander was standing outside.

"Good evening, Mr. Zelenka," he said, rather formally. "I have escorted a guest to Golden Lane who is interested in seeing your work. May we come in?"

Pepik hesitated. "We are quite busy. I really cannot spare the time."

The commander gave him strained smile. "This is a rather special guest."

"All right, then. Come in," sighed Pepik.

The commander entered the little cottage, followed by a person dressed in a long brown cloak that covered him from head to toe. The commander stood at attention as the cloaked figure took in the details of Pepik's cottage: the chair beside the blazing stove, the stack of books piled high on the floor, the flasks and glass vessels perched on the long workbench, and the four children, each at their respective stations, carrying out their part of the Great Work.

When the cloaked figure finished looking around, he nodded. The commander led him further into the room. Five of the emperor's guards followed them.

"And to what do I owe the pleasure of this visit?" asked Pepik. He nervously ran his hand over his head, patting down his straggly hair. "We are quite busy, you know, preparing for tomorrow's demonstration."

The commander gave Pepik a warning look. "Our guest heard of your success today and wished to meet the man responsible for the creation of the white elixir. It has been many years since a feat of this magnitude has been completed in the emperor's court. You have made quite a name for yourself, sir, especially within the walls of the castle."

Pepik coughed and sputtered, not used to receiving such praise. "My goodness, well, I don't know . . . I guess all the conditions were right, and the Lord was with me. If my alembic hadn't cracked, it would have been a glorious day."

"The emperor's court acknowledges that some matters are out of your hands and salutes you just the same."

"The emperor's court?" muttered Uncle Pepik. "The court . . . the . . . Oh!" He looked at the shadowy figure. The commander lifted his finger to his lips so only Pepik and the children could see.

As Josh watched, a transformation came over Pepik. He stood a little taller, his skin took on a rosy glow, and his eyes sparkled. "Well, then, let me explain my approach to you."

The commander escorted the guest over to the workbench. Pepik took a book from the shelf and opened it. "I have studied Sir Roger Bacon's work for many years. This is a copy of his *Speculum Alchemiae*. It is quite rare nowadays, almost impossible to find. I particularly like the way Bacon uses Aristotle's teachings. It is said he was profoundly affected by his reading of *The Secret of Secrets* in 1247.

"In this book, he outlines the preparation of a white and a red elixir, but his elixirs are more powerful than most. One part of his elixir has the potential to transform one thousand parts of metal, as opposed to earlier elixirs that could only transmute at the rate of one to one hundred. The potential of this extra power spurred me on."

The cloaked figure moved in a little closer and tenderly caressed the page with his gloved hand.

Josh leaned over to Ben. "Who is that? He's giving me the creeps."

The person turned and looked in their direction. Even though Josh couldn't see his or her eyes, he could tell they were examining him from head to toe. A sense of relief washed over him when the person turned back to Pepik.

They watched Pepik show his guest around, giving detailed explanations of his equipment, earthenware containers of ingredients, portable charcoal furnace, and other things, all of which were common to an alchemical laboratory. But no matter how eloquent Pepik was in his explanations, the cloaked figure kept wandering back to the *Speculum Alchemiae* and slowly but lovingly turned its pages.

Pepik was about to launch into another detailed explanation of his techniques when the cloaked figure turned to the commander and nodded twice. "I'm sorry to interrupt you, Mr. Zelenka, but we must be on our way. Thank you for your time. May all go well with you tomorrow." The commander ushered the guest and his entourage out and quietly closed the door behind them.

Pepik smiled. "What a day this has been. First, I see the white elixir for the first time in many years, and then this!"

"Who was that?" asked Josh.

"Well, I can't be entirely certain, but I do have some suspicions."

"Come on, don't keep us in suspense. Tell us."

"Well, of course you know the commander."

"Uncle Pepik," groaned Josh.

"And the five guards."

"Come on, tell us who it was."

Pepik burst out laughing. "Oh, Joshua, you are quite a character. You know as well as I do who that was."

"Yes," said Josh, pumping his fist in the air. "I knew it was the emperor."

"Now I know why I recognized his breathing," said Will.

"Yeah, right," scoffed Josh.

"I'm serious. He sounded like the person behind the iron grate when you started the fire."

"Why do you think it's him? I thought the emperor was a recluse," said Ellen.

Pepik smiled. "Although his disguise was excellent, there were several clues. First of all, I assumed he must be someone important because of the trouble he took to hide his identity. If he were a commoner, that wouldn't have been necessary. Second, he wore the finest leather gloves I have ever seen. I know of no one else who would have the money, never mind the connections to obtain such high quality goods."

"You could be a detective, Uncle Pepik," suggested Ellen.

"The commander gave the most important clue, however. Did you notice how he said 'the emperor's court' several times? His choice of words confirmed my suspicions. It is good to see he is on our side. There was certainly no need for him to do that."

Josh began skipping around the room, chanting, "I saw the emperor, I saw the emperor," over and over again. Before long, he was moving so fast that he stopped paying attention to where he was going and crashed into Uncle Pepik's chair. "Oh, my leg," he moaned. "What if it's broken?"

In the midst of all the commotion, Ben ran out the door and stood in the center of the street, watching the emperor and his entourage continue down the lane. Suddenly he ran back into the room. "Uncle Pepik, they've gone to see Scottie."

"And?"

"What if he tries to trick them again?"

"Scottie does not concern me. Have no fear, dear boy. He is already bearing the fruits of his labor." He turned back to his workbench.

"Don't you think we should keep an eye on him?"

Uncle Pepik was so busy fiddling with his alembic that he didn't hear Ben's question.

"Uncle Pepik?"

"Yes," he mumbled, without looking up.

Ben smiled at Josh. "I guess it's okay. Want to join me?"

"Sure."

"Thanks, Uncle," said Ben. He dashed back out the door with Josh limping behind.

Pepik looked up from his work. "Hmm. What was that all about?"

Josh and Ben sneaked along Golden Lane, staying close to the cottages. They ducked whenever they passed a window and hid whenever they heard the slightest noise.

"Are we almost there?" asked Josh.

"It's two houses down. Stay low in case someone comes out," whispered Ben.

They stole over to Scottie's window and peeked in. Scottie was standing in the middle of the floor. Apollo lay at his side, her chin resting on his foot. The emperor was seated on Scottie's tattered velvet chair. The commander sat beside him on a low wooden stool, and the guards stood behind the two of them. Zeus was sprawled on the floor between Scottie and the emperor. Drool dribbled from his mouth, forming a puddle beneath the emperor's feet.

They watched as he leaned over and whispered something to the commander. The commander got up and tried to move Zeus out of the way, but he wouldn't budge. Two of the guards came around and lifted the sleeping dog. He didn't protest as they carried him over to Apollo. The minute his body touched the floor, however, he got up and shook his head—sending slobber everywhere—and then wandered back over to the emperor, settling in even closer.

Scottie began to pace back and forth, completely oblivious to the emperor's dislike of his dog. He lifted various objects off his workbench and handed them to the emperor for his inspection.

"I wonder what he's saying," whispered Josh.

"Let's get closer. If we stand next to the door, we might be able to hear."

They crawled along the cobblestones to the open doorway and pressed their cheeks against the doorjamb so they could listen in. Scottie's voice drifted out to them. "Of course, most alchemists do not appreciate the importance of philosophical mercury, the *argentums vivum*." He held up a sealed glass container containing a reddish liquid. "Its distinctive properties add a certain edge to my preparations, as does my unique athanor." He pointed to the portable furnace resting in one corner. It was made of gold and decorated with hundreds of crystals, the opposite of the sooty black one that Pepik favored.

This time the emperor didn't nod. "I think he's getting bored," whispered Ben. "Everyone knows about philosophical mercury. It's nothing new. His athanor might look better, but it does the same thing."

"Perhaps it is time to show you my most special ingredients," said Scottie. He took down a vial of bubbly lime-green slime. "This is spittle from my rabid wolves. I keep them in a cage out back. You are welcome to see them if you like."

Josh's eyes grew wide." Whoa, did you know about that?" he whispered.

"I've seen them, but they snarl and bite on the bars of the cage whenever anyone comes near, so I never get too close," replied Ben.

The emperor held the vial in his gloved hand and flipped it back and forth, watching its contents swish from one side to the other. His curiosity satisfied, he handed it back to Scottie and waited expectantly, his hands resting on his lap.

"My friends, I am confident I will be able to take your breath

away when you see the beautiful objects I will bring forth next."
Scottie opened a drawer and pulled out a small velvet bag with a
corded drawstring. He carefully loosened the drawstring and dropped
an object about the size of a plum into his hand. A beautiful blue
stone gleamed in the candlelight. "Behold! This stone is from the
sacred bull, Apis, who resides at the temple of Isis and Osiris."

"How did you come to possess it?" asked the commander.

"It was a gift from one of the priests in return for my services."

"Describe these services."

"I made eight hundred drams of the philosopher's stone for them."

"There's no way he could have done that. He's lying," whispered
Ben.

Josh felt goose bumps rise up on his arms and legs. "He's trouble.
We better be careful."

The emperor started to rise from his chair, but Scottie stepped forward and reached out his hand to stop him. Before he could touch the
emperor, one of the guards grabbed him by the arm. "Don't touch the
emperor," he growled.

Scottie jerked his arm away and dusted off his sleeve. "Please, distinguished guest, do not leave. I have several more objects you must
see." He hurried over to his bookshelf and reached behind a stack of
books. "Ah, here it is. I haven't taken this out for some time."

He ran back to the emperor and handed him a small, cloudy glass
container. "Behold, a capsule containing the stingers of queen bees."
The emperor wouldn't acknowledge it. Scottie raced back to the
bookshelf and reached for something else behind a different stack
of books.

"Now we know his hiding spots," whispered Ben.

Scottie lifted out a small ivory case decorated with a delicate pat-
tern of inlaid wood. The emperor undid the clasp, opened the lid, and
lifted out a crystal the size of a ping-pong ball.

"This crystal is used for capturing rays from the constellation
Pleiades," said Scottie, trying to sound confident, but he came across as

anxious. When the emperor didn't respond, he ran over to his bed and pulled out a plain-looking mirror from under his mattress.

"This miraculous piece of glass was found one hundred and fifty years ago in the tomb of a Welsh bishop who was also an adept. A friend of mine, the German alchemist Setonius, gave it to me as a farewell gift. It may look like a simple mirror, but it possesses the ability to reveal things far away. It is said that if you gaze into its depths long enough, you will be able to see amazing things happening in other parts of the world."

Scottie handed the mirror to the commander, who handed it to Rudolph. The emperor inspected it from all sides and tucked it under his cloak. "But . . . But . . . Just a minute . . . What about my mirror?" sputtered Scottie.

"If he tires of it, I shall return it to you," said the commander.

The emperor looked at the commander and nodded twice. They both rose to their feet.

"Please, please, just one more minute. I saved the best for last. I have something you won't want to miss."

The emperor reluctantly sank back down into his seat.

Scottie pulled a leather case out from under his bed. He rushed back to the emperor, taking care not to touch him as he lay the case on his lap.

Ben stuck his head through the doorway, took a quick peek, and pulled it back out before anyone spotted him. "That looks like my uncle's. I wonder where he got it."

The emperor slowly opened the case. "Behold, the horn of a unicorn!" exclaimed Scottie. "This magnificent horn has the power to detect and destroy poisons in one's food. It would be most useful to you, honored guest, as a person of your influence surely would be a frequent target for this sort of treachery."

"That's my uncle's horn! I was wondering where it was," exclaimed Ben.

"How did he get it?" asked Josh.

"He must have taken it when we weren't home. My uncle would never have given it to him. It's one of his prized possessions."

The boys peered in the doorway again.

"Please, let me give you this as a special gift to commemorate your visit to my humble abode," said Scottie.

"He's giving it to the emperor. You'll never get it back," whispered Josh.

"Just watch me," growled Ben. He jumped up and strutted into the room, walked over to the emperor, grabbed the case out of his hands, and slammed it shut.

"This horn belongs to my uncle, Pepik Zelenka. I don't know how Scottie got it, but you can't have it."

The emperor looked at him, stunned. Ben seized the opportunity and ran out of the room with the case tucked under his arm. Josh raced down the street after him.

The guards caught up to them two houses down and dragged them back to the commander. He grabbed them by their shirts and lifted them off the ground. "How dare you upset the emperor and steal his property?"

"That horn belongs to my uncle. Scottie stole it from him. He has no right to give it away," whimpered Ben.

The commander dropped them to the ground. "Is that all you have to say for yourselves?"

Ben nodded.

Just then, the emperor exited the cottage and walked toward his horse-drawn carriage. He stared at Josh and Ben from the depths of his cloak, and then, in a move that surprised everyone, he lifted his hand and made a slicing motion across his throat. There was a moment of shocked silence as the meaning of this gesture dawned on Ben and Josh. They stared at the commander in horror.

The commander held the emperor's gaze for what seemed like an eternity until finally the commander turned away. He swallowed and took a deep breath, but when he spoke, he voice was composed and without emotion. "I'm sorry, but it appears you boys have made a grave mistake. Guards, take them to Daliborka for the night. They will meet the executioner in the morning."

Without further delay, the emperor got into the carriage, and the commander climbed up beside the driver. In an instant they were gone, the clatter of hooves echoing in the darkness.

TEN

A PROMISE

The guards were leading the boys away, with Josh squawking loudly and Ben begging them to let them go, when Pepik burst out of his cottage.

"What trouble have you gotten yourselves into now?" he burbled.

"Uncle, they're going to execute us in the morning," wailed Ben.

"They what?" he asked incredulously.

"The emperor himself ordered their execution. They are to remain at Daliborka for the night," said one of the guards.

All the blood drained from Pepik's face and he started swaying back and forth. "No . . . No . . . This can't be happening. There must be some mistake."

"Uncle, you have to do something. Scottie had your unicorn horn, and I took it back—that's all. I don't want to die," whimpered Ben, his eyes brimming with tears.

"So that's where it went." Pepik reached over and hugged his nephew. "Benjamin, my dear, dear Benjamin, I will go plead with the emperor on your behalf. Perhaps if I explain everything to him he will recant his decision." As he continued talking, Pepik's confidence grew. "Yes, now that I think about it, I am sure this will work. He will be reasonable—he must—you don't just execute eleven-year-old boys for something like this. Lads, come with me. We will speak with His Majesty at once."

"But Uncle Pepik, what about the guards?" said Josh, his arms still pinned behind his back.

"Oh, my, yes, of course. I'm sorry, I'm feeling a bit flustered. Guards, you can release the boys into my care. I will take them to the emperor myself."

The guard holding onto Josh stared at Pepik with disbelief. "You expect us to go against the emperor's orders? You're out of your mind, old man. We serve Rudolph II, the Emperor of Bohemia, and we will not release our prisoners until we receive instructions from His Majesty or the commander to do so."

"But surely you realize this is a terrible mistake."

"It is not my job to question the emperor's orders; it is my job to act on them. Now be off before we arrest you, too."

Pepik stood there, hunched over, wringing his hands together. "Then I shall seek out the emperor at once and get your orders rescinded."

"We've tarried long enough with you. Be on your way," ordered the guard.

"All right, then. I'll be back shortly." Pepik gave the boys a quick hug. "You'll be fine. I'll see to it myself. When I come back, I'll take you home and make you a fresh pot of tripe soup."

"What's tripe?" whispered Josh.

"The stomach of a cow," said Ben.

Josh gave him a weak smile. "Just what I need, cow stomach soup."

"I shall see you at Daliborka within the hour." Pepik turned and ran down the lane toward the emperor's residence as fast as his old legs would take him.

Josh and Ben wriggled, kicked, and yelled at the top of their lungs from their spot on the prison floor. Two more guards carrying a long, thick rope descended the stairs. They grabbed Josh first, hauled him to his feet, and began wrapping the rope around his chest. He responded by wildly thrashing about. Eventually his foot managed to connect with one of the guard's shins. The guard responded by squeezing Josh's wrists tighter. When he wriggled again, the guard jerked his wrists up his back until it felt like his arms were going to break off.

Once he realized that his struggling was getting him nowhere, he forced himself to relax. The guard loosened his grip as he and his partner discussed how to lower Josh down into the underground dungeon.

Sensing an opportunity, Josh lunged forward with all his might, hoping to catch his captors off guard so he could make a quick escape. One of them grabbed him by the shoulder and pushed him back down.

Tears poured down Josh's face. He was so scared he thought he might throw up. "God, please help me. Please don't let me die," he whispered.

His prayer was answered a minute later when Pepik burst into the room. "Oh, good—here you are," he said between gasps. "They wouldn't let me see the emperor, and I couldn't find the commander."

Even bigger tears rolled down Josh's cheeks. He choked back a sob. "What's going to happen to us? I don't want to die." He began crying so hard that his nose started to run. He twisted his neck as far as he could, but he couldn't quite manage to wipe his nose on his shoulder.

"This is terrible, just terrible, an absolute travesty," moaned Pepik. "Guards, what should I do? Do you know where I can find the commander?"

"Go look for him yourself," said the head guard.

"Where's your compassion? These boys don't deserve this."

"That is not our concern. We serve the emperor, not you. If you continue to disrupt our work, we will have no choice but to remove you from this room."

The conversation dwindled to nothing when Scottie made his entrance into the room. He held a leash in each hand, and his cape billowed out behind him as the dogs tugged him along. Apollo and Zeus were more interested in dragging him wherever they wanted to go than in obeying his commands. Drool flung in every direction as they towed Scottie across the floor.

"Sit!" he hollered. Apollo fell to the floor and Zeus reluctantly sat down beside her.

"Well, well, what do we have here? I was rather surprised when I looked out my window and saw my old neighbor running down the lane. I didn't know you could move that fast," he snickered. "When I went to your cottage, the others told me you had gone in this direction, so I hurried over. Will agreed to monitor my furnace so I could make some enquiries on your behalf."

He transferred both leashes into one hand and slapped Pepik on the back. "I see your rogue apprentices have gotten themselves into quite a mess this time."

"It's all your fault!" shouted Ben. "You're the one who took my uncle's horn in the first place."

Scottie pretended he didn't hear Ben's outburst. "When is their execution scheduled for?"

"The morning," admitted Pepik reluctantly.

"It appears you don't have much time to rectify this dreadful situation."

"I already ran to the emperor's residence, but they wouldn't let me see him or the commander. I don't know what else to do. I would do anything for these boys, but I fear they are lost."

"Hmm," said Scottie. He cocked his head to one side and stared at Josh and Ben. "Perhaps we can make a deal." He gave Pepik a sly smile, revealing his crooked yellow teeth. "How important is it that you see the emperor?"

"Very important," said Pepik, his head bobbing up and down. "I would do anything to free these boys. They don't deserve to be executed. But what can you possibly do? You hardly bear the court's favor after your recent trickery. Why, I myself have no reason to trust you."

"The commander owes me a favor. Just the other day, I obtained a certain concoction for him, an elixir of sorts, that cured his wife of dropsy. While he paid me heartily for it," he added, jiggling the pouch of coins in his pocket, "I believe I could persuade him to have the boys released."

"Why, thank you, my friend, thank you," said Pepik. He grabbed Scottie and gave him a big kiss on each cheek.

Scottie squirmed out of Pepik's grasp and took a step back, putting some distance between them. "Dear Pepik, before you get too carried away, you must realize that I expect something in return."

"Of course. What would you like? Anything I have is yours."

"In several hours, we have another presentation of our craft. You came very close to making the stone yesterday. I was impressed, as was the emperor. As the preeminent alchemists on the lane, you and I are expected to go first in the morning. The rest of the alchemists from the lane will present in the afternoon."

"What do you want, Scottie?" interrupted Pepik.

"If I am able to secure the release of the boys, all I ask is that if you create the stone tomorrow, you give me your portion of it."

"I value the lives of these precious children more than anything. All I have is yours."

"Very well. This is a good deal for both of us. Your chances of succeeding are so slight that our little exchange will probably cost you nothing."

Pepik nervously ran his hand over his head. "And what if I create the stone and the emperor takes it all for himself? Then what?"

"You know the protocol as well as I do. When an alchemist creates the stone, they always give the largest portion to their patron. That is part of our agreement."

"But our situation is different. Rudolph is mad. It would not be out of character for him to take it all."

"If that happens, there is nothing you or I can do about it. It is only if you get a portion of the stone for yourself that you must give it to me. Is that clear?"

"My only concern is for the boys. I will give you my share if anything comes of my work."

"Then we have a deal," said Scottie. They shook hands, he gave his dogs a command, and the three of them sauntered out.

They were barely out the door when Pepik walked over to the head guard and whispered something to him.

The guard looked at Pepik and then at the boys. "Are you mad?"

Pepik leaned over and whispered something more.

The guard shook his head. "Are you sure that's what you want to do?"

Pepik nodded.

"All right then." He muttered something to his co-workers and left the room.

Thirty minutes later, the commander stalked into the prison followed by a group of guards. He opened the grate and stared down the hole. It was so dark he couldn't see a thing. "Are they in there?" he asked.

"Yes, as you ordered, sir," replied one of the guards.

"Two of them?"

"Yes, sir, two eleven-year-old boys. They cried at first, but for the last few minutes they have been quiet. Perhaps they are sleeping."

"Release them."

"Yes, sir."

One of the guards called out instructions to the boys; a rope was quickly lowered down the hole, and minutes later Josh was lifted out. His shirt and breeches were rumpled and dirty, and his face stained with tears. He ran over to Pepik, sobbing, and wrapped his arms around the alchemist's plump chest.

"You're fine, lad, just fine." Pepik stroked Josh's hair and murmured soothing words of encouragement as they waited for Ben to be hoisted up.

"How did you get us out?" asked Josh between sniffles.

"Oh, just a bit of negotiating, that's all. It wasn't too difficult."

Once both boys were firmly in his grasp, Pepik led them out of the prison and walked them back to his cottage on Golden Lane.

"Josh! Ben! You're back," cried Ellen. She ran over to her brother and gave him a hug. "I was getting so worried, especially after Scottie came here and told us what had happened. Are you okay?"

"I think so, although it was pretty scary in that dungeon. I heard all kinds of scratching noises. I think there were rats," said Josh.

"Good thing Will wasn't with you. He would have hated that."

"Where is he?"

"He's still at Scottie's. He should be back any minute. How come you got out?"

"I don't know. Uncle Pepik said something about negotiating."

Pepik walked over to them. "Children, I hate to interrupt your chitchat, but we must hurry. In four hours we have to be at Powder Tower, and there is much work to be done."

"No problem, Uncle Pepik. What would you like us to do?" asked Ben.

"Ellen, continue to monitor the athanor. We need to reduce its output by about one tenth. Josh, pack up the supplies. Ben, you and Will can complete one more distillation. We must hurry because we are not nearly as far as we were yesterday."

"Don't worry, Uncle. We'll help you catch up," said Ben.

"That remains to be seen, dear lad. Our experiments are difficult to duplicate at the best of times, and we missed hours of work with our troubles last night. Whatever will be will be. We're in the Lord's hands now."

— ELEVEN —

THE SHOWDOWN

CRGUGGCRGUGGCRGUGGCRGUG

The children trudged down Golden Lane carrying crates of alchemy equipment and supplies. This time they knew what to expect, so they were able to reduce their load by half. Pepik led the way carrying his three most reliable alembics; Ellen had his ancient copy of *Speculum Alchemiae* tucked under her arm; Will lugged a crate of herbs and other dried matter; and Josh and Ben carefully carried a full cucurbit, fresh from the athanor, wrapped in a blanket so it wouldn't cool on the journey.

They were barely out the door when Josh stepped on the back of Ellen's heel. "Ouch! Watch where you're going," she cried.

"I can't see over this stupid thing. How was I supposed to know your heel was in my way?" he muttered.

"No, your foot was in my way."

Uncle Pepik turned toward them and continued walking down the lane backwards. "My goodness, are you fighting already? The day has barely begun."

"But she's driving me crazy," protested Josh.

"Now, now," said Pepik.

"Uncle Pepik," interupted Ben, "you'd better—"

Pepik took another step backward. His heel connected with a small fence that surrounded a flower garden. He was so startled that he let go of his cargo as he fell backward. The alembics crashed to the ground, sending bits of glass everywhere. Pepik landed on a patch of daisies, his feet straight up in the air, groaning.

Seconds later, people up and down the lane were sticking their heads out their cottage doors and windows. Some pointed and laughed, but most gave Pepik pitying looks before going back to their business.

Josh and Ben put down their cucurbit and ran over to him. "Are you all right?" asked Josh.

Pepik pushed the daisies away from his face and smiled. "My ample backside protected me when I fell, but I fear the alembics are beyond hope. Help me up, boys. We'll go back and get a few more."

Josh helped him to his feet, taking care to avoid the broken glass. "Why do I have a feeling things aren't going to go well today?" he muttered.

The laboratory in Powder Tower had been returned to its pristine state. Not a sliver of glass or drop of Pepik's white elixir remained. Identical sets of athanors, alembics, crucibles, and the other necessities had been set up on two tables placed on opposite sides of the room. Guards were stationed behind each work area to ensure that no trickery would take place.

Scottie had arrived earlier and staked out his territory first. He was busy organizing his equipment on the left side of the room. Apollo and Zeus sat on the floor beside him like a pair of sphinxes. They watched Pepik, Ellen, and Will enter the room but didn't move a muscle.

"Well, well, if it isn't the old man and his motley crew of misfits, although it's a smaller crew this morning, I see. I'm surprised you decided to come. Under the circumstances, I thought this would be the last place you would be. I expected you to be pleading with the commander, seeing as I failed, or mourning the fate of your boys at

Daliborka." He shrugged his shoulders. "I obviously underestimated your competitive spirit."

Scottie stopped his blustering when Josh and Ben walked in carrying the cucurbit. At the sight of the boys, all the blood drained from his face. "What? They're still alive? How did you manage to obtain their release?"

"I suppose you could say the commander changed his mind," said Pepik, not looking up from the crate he was unpacking.

"Why? When I spoke to him, he said Rudolph was adamant that the boys remain at Daliborka and be executed this morning. There was no room for negotiation."

Pepik shrugged his shoulders. "It is of no consequence. The main thing is that they are in my trusty care." He looked over at Josh and Ben. Josh returned his kindly gaze with a grateful smile.

Just then the commander entered the room, followed by a squad of the emperor's guards. Scottie clapped his hands together. "Oh, good. Commander, you are here just in time. There is a great mystery I am trying to solve. Perhaps you can shed some light on this interesting turn of events."

"What now, Scotta?" asked the commander.

"When I spoke with you this morning, you indicated there was no possible way the boys would be released from Daliborka, yet now I find them here, assisting my, um, shall I say, 'colleague.' Did our mad emperor have a change of heart?"

"If I were you, Scotta, I'd watch my words carefully. His Majesty has eyes and ears everywhere. Regarding the boys, I released them once Pepik volunteered to exchange his life for theirs. Of course, if Pepik produces the stone today, all will be forgotten."

For a moment, Josh felt like his heart stopped beating. "You did what?" he gasped.

Uncle Pepik looked down at the floor.

Josh's eyes filled with tears. He ran over and gave Pepik a hug. Ben, Will, and Ellen quickly followed.

Scottie stalked over to them and pulled the children away. "Have you gone mad? What on earth would possess you to do such a thing?"

Pepik looked away. He wouldn't say a word.

Finally the commander broke the silence. "His Majesty will be here shortly. Finish your preparations so we can begin."

Josh and Pepik had just heated the athanor to the correct temperature when they heard the sound of footsteps coming up the stone staircase. "All rise," shouted the commander.

Josh put down his metal shovel and stood up straight, his arms rigid at his sides.

Six guards entered the room, followed by the emperor and his large entourage. The emperor was wrapped in a black velvet cloak that extended past his fingertips and dragged on the floor behind him. Underneath the cloak, he wore the strangest looking outfit: a fitted red top with gold threads running through it and a pair of puffy shorts. A pair of white hose, black ankle boots, and a gold medallion necklace completed the outfit.

The emperor's jeweled crown only partially covered his hair, which was falling out in large patches and hung in greasy strands in front of his eyes. He reached up and self-consciously rubbed the rash on his cheeks as he stared at Pepik and Scottie.

Josh was so surprised by the emperor's appearance that he started to giggle. The emperor gave him an arrogant sneer and slipped his hand under his shirt, beneath his armpit, and pumped his elbow up and down. Josh turned beet red and looked away.

The emperor turned to the two alchemists. "Which of you is the one who gave me the mirror?"

"It wasn't exactly a gift, Your Majesty. When you are through with it, I would welcome its return, but please keep it as long as you like," said Scottie.

"It was a useless piece of junk. I had it burned." The emperor jerked his head to one side. One of his aides ran over with a heavily carved wooden stool. He plopped down onto it. "Begin."

"Who would you like to go first, Your Majesty?" asked the commander.

The emperor pointed to Scottie.

"All right, then. Scotta, proceed."

Scottie added a few coals to the fire burning on his hearth and used his bellows to fan them into flame.

"I can't see," moaned the emperor. Two of the guards picked up his stool and carried him closer to Scottie.

Scottie turned and faced the emperor. "I will be creating the philosopher's stone, or red elixir as some call it, using the dry method. I realize this is an unusual approach. Its very existence is not acknowledged by many practitioners of our art, but I have chosen this method because of its great simplicity and speed. It requires less time, materials, and schooling.

"Before you arrived, I placed two substances in my crucible: celestial salt and a terrestrial metallic body. The celestial salt, also called philosophical mercury, is from a secret source I cannot and will not name, but you would be close if you thought it came from an adept in Avignon—the very same Avignon where Pope John XXII was rumored to have done his transmutations. It is said he accumulated twenty-five million drams of gold, an unbelievable fortune for a man of the cloth. I cleaned the philosophical mercury with saltpeter to ensure its absolute purity.

"The terrestrial metallic body I have chosen was harvested under auspicious conditions from the depths of the earth. Again, it was obtained by mysterious means, so please do not ask me about its origin. You would be close, however, if you thought it was found in a secret passage in an ancient Alexandrian temple, collected by the sister of a famous alchemist."

Scottie put his wand into the crucible and slowly stirred.

Josh glanced over at the emperor. He was sitting there, his eyes glazed, twiddling his thumbs. Scottie seemed totally unaware of the emperor's boredom and jabbered on as he continued stirring.

"The dry method, which until now has been obscured by a thick veil, requires only the simple crucible. No alembic, no cucurbit, no luting, no athanor—you must admit, it is a superior process."

He leaned over and peered into his earthenware container. Suddenly his hand flew to his mouth and he let out a gasp. "Oh, my. The colors of the peacock's tail—they flashed by so quickly. Your Majesty, look!"

Josh jumped to his feet. He was standing next to Scottie, looking into his crucible, before the emperor could even get up. The molten metal in Scottie's crucible was covered with flecks of gold.

"Voilá! It is done. Behold, the philosopher's stone!" shouted Scottie.

The emperor looked into the crucible. He was so pleased by what he saw that he bounced up and down on his tiptoes. "That was magnificent," he exclaimed breathlessly. He motioned for the commander to come over. Josh watched as he lifted the crucible off the coals and carried it to a nearby workbench.

Another wave of joy overtook the emperor. "Oh my. Oh my. Oh my," he gasped. He stopped bouncing for a second and gave Scottie a heart-melting smile. "Do it again."

All the blood drained from Scottie's face for the second time that morning, and a wet sheen coated his brow. He took a deep breath. "Your Majesty, from all your years of study you know as well as I do that our experiments can rarely be duplicated. Why, it would be impossible to replicate the exact conditions that were present in the heavens a minute ago, and furthermore, I used all of my philosophical mercury for this presentation. I am sorry, Your Majesty, but I cannot fulfill your request."

The emperor tilted his head to one side. "You cannot or will not?" he asked with a hint of menace in his voice.

The commander stalked over to the emperor and whispered into his ear. A terrible look came over Rudolph's face—a brief glimpse of sadness that was swiftly replaced with a hateful stare. His eyes narrowed to tiny slits and his lips seemed to curl outward, giving him the appearance of a rabid dog. Even Apollo and Zeus sensed that something was amiss. They awoke from their naps, lifted their heads, and stared at the emperor.

The commander walked over to Scottie. Five guards followed and took up their positions behind him. He looked Scottie square in the eye. "Is there something you would like to tell the emperor?"

"But . . . Well . . . Why . . . I have no idea what you are talking about."

"I think you do. I'll give you one more chance. Is there something you would like to tell His Majesty before it is too late?"

Scottie stood there, motionless, except for his Adam's apple, which continued to bob up and down. His eyes roamed the room as he looked for a way to escape. Apollo and Zeus stood up and lumbered over to him.

"Well?"

"Yes, there is one thing I would like to say. I would be happy to repeat my presentation for the emperor, but I need several weeks to prepare, as it is difficult to obtain philosophical mercury. I would be happy to honor His Majesty's request, given the appropriate amount of time."

"May I inspect your crucible?" asked the commander.

"But . . . Well . . . Why would you want to do that?"

The commander ignored his question. He took one of the emperor's crucibles off a nearby shelf and set it next to Scottie's. They appeared to be identical, but on closer inspection, the clay in Scottie's was slightly darker. The commander poured Scottie's molten gold into the empty crucible and inspected the bottom of his original one. "Ah, just as I expected, a thin ring of wax. He used a wax bottom to hide his gold filings."

"What? There must be some mistake. I would never resort to such treachery."

"Save your breath, fool. You've been caught red-handed again. Guards, take him to Daliborka. We'll deal with him shortly."

Scottie lurched forward and tried to make a run for the door, but the guards quickly blocked his path. Apollo responded by clamping her jaws down on one of the guards' legs. The man let out a horrible cry of pain. His co-workers rushed over and tried to pry Apollo off of him. In the midst of the commotion, the commander led the emperor away from the melee and stood in front of him to protect him from the fighting.

Suddenly the anguished cry of a different guard got everyone's attention. Zeus had pinned him to the ground and stood on top of him, growling fiercely as he dripped great globs of drool onto his face. Two guards ran over and tried to pull Zeus off, but he wouldn't move. One of them thrust the blade of his sword into Zeus's front leg. A spurt of blood gushed out, but it didn't slow him one bit. He lunged again, his great body flying through the air, and knocked two more guards to the ground.

With everyone distracted, Scottie saw his opportunity and slipped out the door. Apollo and Zeus didn't miss a beat. They stopped attacking the guards and hurried out after their master, their furry tails standing as straight as flagpoles as they disappeared out the door. The commander shouted out an order and four guards raced after them.

With the fighting over, the commander led the emperor back to his chair, stepping carefully to avoid the puddles of drool and blood. Once he was comfortable, everyone returned to their places.

"All right, Zelenka, I believe we are ready for your presentation," said the commander. "I sincerely hope you can do better. Your life depends upon it."

TWELVE

THE PHILOSOPHER'S STONE

⊂⊃⊰⊱⊂⊃⊰⊱⊂⊃⊰⊱⊂⊃⊰⊱

Pepik slowly walked over to his equipment, his head hung low. He stood behind the athanor and watched his alembic bubble away for a second before falling to his knees. The room was silent as everyone watched him pray. After several minutes he struggled to his feet, his knees creaking as he stood up. He examined the white liquid in his alembic before looking up at the emperor.

"Your Majesty, I imagine you were told that I created the white elixir yesterday. I am most appreciative of your excellent equipment and supplies. Thank you."

The emperor nodded.

"While I realize that some alchemists prefer the short, dry method that Scottie tried to demonstrate, I myself have been a fan of the wet method for over fifty years. After the unfortunate accident with my alembic yesterday, I worked very hard, despite many interruptions." He looked at Josh and Ben and winked. "By the grace of God, I managed to recreate the legendary white elixir again. That in itself is a miracle, as any good alchemist like yourself would know. Our work usually takes months of arduous labor, and even then there is no guarantee of success."

The emperor rolled his eyes and waved his hand in the air. "Get on with it."

Pepik blushed fiercely. "Yes, Your Majesty." He heaped more coals in the athanor and pumped air at them with the bellows until they glowed. "If all goes well, God willing, I believe that with enough heat, the white elixir, which is based on the *prima material*, that from which all things were created, will change color before our eyes until it reaches its purest state—that of the red elixir, the philosopher's stone. Ben, please come assist me with the bellows."

Ben hurried over and continued feeding an even stream of air over the coals. The room began to heat up as the furnace burned hotter and hotter. The emperor gave his cloak to the commander and placed his crown on his lap.

Pepik leaned over the cucurbit, desperately hoping something would happen. "Harder Ben, blow harder," he commanded. Ben pumped the bellows as fast as he could. Pepik closed his eyes, concentrating so hard that his face contorted into a mass of wrinkles as he prayed.

The alembic kept bubbling away.

Suddenly Pepik clutched his hand to his heart. "Of course! How could I forget?" He rummaged through his pocket, muttering away to himself.

"What are you doing?" demanded the emperor. "You're wasting my time."

Pepik grunted triumphantly as he pulled a tiny piece of gold out of his pocket, not even half the size of Josh's baby fingernail. "I almost forgot the ferment, but thankfully the Lord brought my blunder to mind."

"Ferment? What are you talking about, you old puffer?" demanded the emperor.

"Yesterday I reread my most obscure alchemy text, one written by Zosimus of Panopolis, who lived in Egypt around 300 A.D. He wrote that every metal is striving to reach the perfection of gold. If we add a small quantity of gold to our work it will act as a catalyst. It speeds up the natural process, you know, just as a bit of yeast raises a great quantity of dough."

"We've seen enough trickery for one day, Zelenka. How are we to know that this is not more of the same?" asked the commander.

"For one thing, I'm showing you this gold, not hiding it like Scottie did. And second, this idea was documented over a thousand years ago. Surely that in itself would be proof."

The commander looked at the emperor. He was sitting on his stool, his nose pinched between his two index fingers, staring at Pepik through half-closed eyes.

"Your Majesty, may I proceed with the ferment?" asked Pepik.

"Yes."

Pepik unwound the lute-soaked cloth that connected his glass vessels, took them apart, dropped the gold into the cucurbit, and put his equipment back together. He took a step back so he wouldn't block the emperor's view, closed his eyes, and resumed his prayers.

"Uncle, look," interrupted Ben.

Pepik's eyes popped open. "Your Majesty, look!" he shouted.

The emperor lurched forward, followed by the commander, Josh, Will, and Ellen. They huddled around the glass and watched as the white elixir turned iridescent, like the colors on a peacock's tail. A bright yellow seeped through the mixture, tinting it pale yellow. Once all the liquid had taken on that hue, it continued changing, growing deeper and deeper, until it resembled the vivid yellow of a wild buttercup growing in a country meadow.

Josh stood there, spellbound, not daring to breathe. Ben pumped the bellows even faster, spurred on by the miraculous sight. They watched the color shift to orange, again slowly filtering through the mixture, changing from bright yellow to pale orange to medium orange, until it was bright orange like a pumpkin. It paused at that shade for a second and then moved through a range of purples, not settling until it was the deep purple of an eggplant. Once that color was complete, a rich, brilliant red flooded the mixture in one enormous burst.

The children were hooting and hollering and jumping up and down when suddenly a violent hissing noise erupted from the cucurbit in staccato-like bursts. The red elixir in the cucurbit exploded, sending a stream of condensation into the alembic. A beautiful aroma filled the room. It was the most wonderful smell you could imagine: the combination of a dewy spring morning tinged with the perfume of a fresh rose, the breath of wind on a mountaintop, and the scent of the warm earth in a garden after a summer rain.

The instant the condensation entered the alembic, it cooled into a thick, robust, deeply colored scarlet liquid. Light sparkled off of it like gold. The emperor was so pleased that he clapped.

"Oh, my," said Pepik. "At last, the *opus magnum*. I never thought I would have the honor of witnessing the Great Work again in my lifetime."

Josh's jaw dropped. "You've seen this before?"

"Most men dream of seeing it just once in their life. I have been blessed twice. The stone is as beautiful today as it was thirty-seven years ago."

Josh was standing there, admiring Pepik's creation, when a quiet whisper caught his attention. The emperor was gently stroking the alembic as he bobbed up and down on his tiptoes.

"It's mine," he whispered, "all mine. Wealth—eternal life—all within my grasp." He rubbed his hands together as he stared at the red liquid.

Pepik frowned. "Is that all this means to you?"

"What?" said the emperor, clearly annoyed that Pepik had interrupted him.

Pepik took a step closer so their faces were inches apart. "Why do you need more wealth? You have more than most people could even dream of, and you've wasted most of it on worthless trinkets. Do you really believe that having more money will make you happier?"

"Commander, remove this man. He's bothering me," whined the emperor.

"And what of your health, Your Majesty? Look at you. Your hair is falling out in clumps, your face is covered in a terrible rash, and you're losing your mind. You've wasted your days, consumed by whatever you think will satisfy your endless cravings."

For a minute it looked like the emperor was going to cry, but a wicked smile flashed across his face instead. "How dare you speak to me like that? I ought to feed you to my lion," he snarled.

Pepik responded by grabbing the alembic by its long, skinny neck and throwing it to the ground. It exploded before it hit the floor, sending shards of glass and droplets of elixir everywhere.

The commander stared at Pepik, dumbfounded.

As Pepik surveyed the damage, he smiled.

"How dare you?" shouted the emperor, hopping up and down. "That elixir was the property of my kingdom. You had no right to destroy it."

"Your Majesty, look," said the commander, pointing to the floorboards. Every single nail the elixir touched had turned to gold. Long rows of golden nails gleamed in the sunlight that flooded through the windows.

The emperor fell to the floor, grabbed several large chunks of glass, and began licking them off. When they were clean he ran his tongue over the floorboards, slurping up any drops of liquid he could find. He cut his tongue in the process, and soon the floor was tinted with the red elixir and the emperor's blood.

The emperor lifted his head just long enough to give one last command. "Bring my lion here at once. He needs to get his share before it's completely gone."

THIRTEEN

THE MOTTO

Pepik and the children sneaked out of the laboratory and returned to their cottage on Golden Lane.

"Uncle Pepik, why did you do it? You finally made the philosopher's stone, and then you destroyed it. Why?" asked Ben.

"Since I was sponsored by the emperor he had a right to whatever I made, but when I saw him stroking my alembic, I realized that the whole thing was wrong. The emperor has been miserable for years. He has more than most people could ever dream of, yet it's never enough. Giving him more money or a longer life wouldn't make him any happier, although he doesn't realize it. When I thought about what I'd made and the power it possessed, I realized that it brought out the worst in the emperor instead of the best."

"Why didn't you tell us you made the stone before?" asked Will.

"I didn't think it was necessary for you to know."

"There were a bunch of times I felt like giving up. If I had known you had made it before, I would have tried a lot harder," said Ben.

"Well, it doesn't matter now. It's over."

"What are we going to do?" asked Josh.

"We need to leave Prague immediately. Once the emperor is done with the elixir, I am certain he will want to punish me. It's time to move on; I've been here long enough. We'll journey to my sister's home. It's about a three-hour walk from here. She lives outside the city. I can always count on her for a fine meal and a place to sleep."

Josh licked his lips. "That sounds great. I'm starving."

"Imagine that," said Ellen.

"Hey, come on. I know you're hungry, too. We haven't had a decent meal in days."

Uncle Pepik frowned.

"Oops, sorry," said Josh.

"It's all right, lad. I know I'm not much of a cook. Help me grab a few of my things. We better hurry. The guards will be coming soon."

After a long walk through the countryside, past rolling hills and fields lush with the new growth of spring, Pepik and the children came upon his sister's house. It was at the end of a long, winding path that branched off the main road.

Her quaint little home was set amidst an orchard of fruit trees. The minute she heard their voices she rushed out, her ample body jiggling up and down as she ran to greet them.

"Ah, Pepik," she said, folding him into her arms, "It's so good to see you. And Benjamin, you, too," she added, patting him on the head. "You've grown. And look, you've brought some friends. Come in, I shall prepare a feast for the five of you."

"My aunt's a great cook," said Ben. "You're in for a treat."

The kids explored the orchard and surrounding woods and played a game of tag while Pepik's sister cooked the meal. When it was time to eat, Pepik called them into the house. They sat on long wooden benches that surrounded a rustic farmhouse table.

Pepik prayed, and then his sister gave the instructions. "Come now, don't be shy. Dig in."

Josh heaped his plate with food and tucked right into it. He started with a bowl of Moravian cabbage soup with sausage and a side dish of smoked ox tongue with dill sauce. The main course was meat,

meat, and more meat—a challenge for Ellen—so she stuck to the dumplings, fried cheese with potatoes and tartar sauce, and finger rolls. Pepik's sister had prepared roast duck, roast neck of pork, veal sausage, dumplings, and cabbage. Everything was so delicious that before long even Josh, who was always hungry, was so full that he actually declined the offer of seconds and thirds when the food was passed around again. Just when he thought he couldn't eat another bite, Pepik's sister came out with a plate of pancakes filled with fruit preserves.

When their feast was finished, Pepik leaned back from the table and passed wind.

"Why, thank you, brother," said his sister.

He smiled at her, looking more relaxed than he had in days. "That was a delicious meal. *Thank you.*" Josh, Will, and Ellen stared at them with astonishment.

Josh leaned over to Ben. "Are you allowed to pass gas at the table?"

"Of course. My aunt likes it if we pass gas. That way she knows we got enough to eat."

Josh giggled. He sat there as still as he could and tried to offer Pepik's sister a big thank you, but all that came out was a tiny little blurp. Fortunately, what it lacked in volume it made up for in smell.

"Josh, what are you doing? Excuse yourself," scolded Ellen.

"But Ben said we're supposed to pass gas to say thank you."

"What?"

"It's true. Ben told me."

She grimaced. "I'm not doing that."

"It sounds good to me. Thank you, madam. That was a great meal," said Will.

"Yes, thanks too, Auntie. It was great, as always. I wish you'd teach Uncle how to cook," said Ben. By the time he and Will had added their thanks, the room smelled like rotten cabbage.

"You know, I thought Czechoslovakian food was terrible, but now I know it was just your uncle's cooking," said Josh.

When Ben and Ellen got up to help with the dishes, Will scooted down the bench to his brother. "Josh, do you have the time stone?"

"I haven't seen it. Have you?"

"No. I'm getting kind of worried. We should be going home soon."

"It'll come when it's supposed to. Just relax. Our journey must not be done yet. We must have something else to do or the stone would be here by now."

Ellen walked back to the table and gathered another armful of dishes. "What's up?" she asked.

"Will's worried about the stone. He thinks it's time to go home," said Josh.

Ellen put down the dishes. "Let's go talk with Uncle Pepik."

They found him outside, sitting in the sun.

"Ah, this feels good—a welcome change after all those hours in my dark laboratory. Come join me."

The three of them sat down on the soft grass beside him.

"Uncle Pepik, I have some questions," said Josh.

"Really? Imagine that," he replied, with just a hint of a smile. "Go on."

"I feel really confused about this alchemy stuff. I keep wondering why you think alchemy will help you grow close to God. That's not what they teach us in church."

"And . . ." said Pepik.

"You told us that all these different people from the church practiced it and wrote about it and all that other stuff. I keep wondering how a crook like Scottie can be included with them."

"And . . ."

"You know what bugs me the most? The fact that you didn't tell us you made the stone before. You could have stopped Scottie from making fun of you, and the commander and the emperor would have treated you better, but you let everyone mock you because they didn't know the truth."

"Hmm."

There was a long silence as Pepik pondered his questions. Josh began to worry that he had offended him.

"Let's start with your last question first. The reason I didn't tell anyone that I made the stone before is because I didn't think it would do any good. If Scottie knew, he would have driven me crazy trying to learn my secrets. If the emperor knew, he would have locked me in his tower and expected me to produce it on demand. And as for me, I prefer not to talk about it because I was going through such a terrible time when I first made it. I had hoped to create the philosopher's stone in time to save my dying son, but the Great Work wasn't complete until a few weeks after his death. Those were such sad times for me, losing my wife and son." Pepik's eyes filled with tears. "I try not to think about it."

"Oh," said Josh, feeling guilty. "Sorry."

"It's not your fault, dear boy. The Lord giveth and the Lord taketh. Blessed be the name of the Lord."

"What did you do with the first stone you made?" asked Will.

"I gave it to the church to use for the construction of St. Paul's Basilica in Rome. It's expensive building a cathedral, you know."

"You helped build the basilica?" exclaimed Will.

"I gave them what the Lord gave me, that's all."

Josh, Will, and Ellen looked at him with new appreciation.

"And back to your second question, yes, it bothers me that a crook like Scottie is involved in alchemy. He gives all alchemists a bad name. Unfortunately, there are frauds and cheats in every occupation, whether it's the butcher who gives you less meat than you paid for or the mystic who makes up visions to make himself look good. We reap what we sow. I believe the Lord will give Scottie what he deserves."

Two birds flew overhead, chirping away as they settled in a nearby tree. Josh looked at his brother. "Just think, you wanted to go with him."

Will blushed and turned away.

Pepik gave Will a wistful smile. "An old friend of mine once said, 'If anyone has a powerful enemy he dare not attack openly, he should instead recommend the study of alchemy, for that will surely ruin him.' Scottie's life illustrates this principle well."

"I never thought of it that way," said Josh.

Just then Ben wandered out and joined them. "What are you doing?" he asked.

"I'm giving our friends another alchemy lesson. Now, Josh, your first question—how alchemy draws us closer to God—is a rather complicated one. Before I answer, there is something I need to tell you, something very few people know about me."

The four of them leaned in closer.

"Before I married my wife, Danica, I was a monk."

"What?" gasped Ben, his eyes as big as saucers. "Why didn't you tell me that before?"

"I didn't think you needed to know. Many of the monks in the monastery where I lived were adepts. We saw many similarities between alchemy and our faith."

"Like what?" asked Will.

"Just as metal seeks to become gold, we strive to become better people—more like our example, Jesus Christ, and grow in our faith."

"That makes sense," said Josh.

"Our motto, '*oro, lege, relege, labora, et invenis,*' or 'pray, read, reread, work, and you shall find' can apply to our walk with God as well. That's why Jesus said, 'Ask and it will be given to you; seek and you will find; knock and the door will be opened to you. For everyone who asks receives; he who seeks finds; and to him who knocks, the door will be opened.'

"When we believe, the Lord works in our hearts to transform us into the kind of people he wants us to be, but he also expects us to participate in the process. If we *pray*, *read*, and *reread* the Bible and *work* at becoming the kind of people God wants us to be, we *shall find* him and learn to know him in a deeper, better way."

"Whoa, that's good. I like that," exclaimed Josh. "I'm going to remember that: 'pray, read, reread, work, and you shall find.'"

"The other reason I like alchemy is because of the symbolism. For me, the philosopher's stone reminds me of Jesus. When it is combined with base metal, which I think of as a person like me, it turns metal into gold. Jesus can have that same kind of transforming power in my life. He can make me more like him, more precious than gold."

"The red elixir could remind you of his blood, too. My dad always says that Jesus' death on the cross—you know, his blood—that's what has the power to change us," said Josh.

"I must say, you are a smart young man. I knew the minute I set eyes on you that you'd be an excellent alchemist."

Josh grinned from ear to ear.

"You do realize, however, that being an alchemist is a big commitment. You have to live your life in keeping with our beliefs and principles. If you don't, you'll be like Scottie and give us all a bad name. Make sure you're ready for this before you take it further," said Pepik.

"That's the same as being a Christian. How we live tells others what we believe about God," interjected Will.

"My goodness, you are just as smart as your brother."

Will grimaced. "No, actually I'm smarter."

Josh cuffed him on the arm. "I've never thought of it like that, Uncle Pepik, but it's true. If you say you are a Christian, but you don't read your Bible or pray or try to live your life in a way that pleases God, what you're really saying is that God isn't very important to you."

"I agree. If we live right and honor God with every part of our lives, that tells people that we take God seriously," added Ellen.

Pepik smiled. "Imagine, three of you that are so insightful, and from one family—impressive, I must say. I would like to add one final thought to all of this. Don't worry about what others say or think about your life. Worry about what God thinks, and the rest will take care of itself."

They nodded in agreement.

"I have one more question, Uncle Pepik," said Ellen.

"What is that, my dear?"

"What are you going to do now?"

"Actually, I was thinking that Ben and I needed to take a little trip, a pilgrimage of sorts. I was thinking about heading to Rome to see the basilica and visit my friends at the monastery. What do you think, Ben? Would you like to come?"

"Of course, Uncle. That would be great."

"What about us? Can we come, too?" asked Josh.

"Well, I suppose. I will happily take you, but it will require months of walking to get there."

"I'm good with that," said Josh.

"Me, too," said Ellen.

Will didn't say anything.

Josh leaned back and stretched, absentmindedly running his hands through the grass behind him. Suddenly his fingers connected with something round and smooth. He grabbed it and lifted it up, knowing full well what he had just found, let out a big sigh, and sat up and smiled.

"What?" said Will. "What's going on?"

Josh slowly unfurled his fingers. The time stone lay on his palm, its third symbol already beginning to fade.

"Guys," he said, "we're going home."

Josh woke up on the floor in his bedroom, with Will and Ellen sprawled out on either side of him. He lay there for a minute with a smile on his face. *"Oro, lege, relege, labora, et invenis,"* he whispered. "Pray, read, reread, work, and you shall find."

THE END.

"Therefore, since we are surrounded by
such a huge crowd of witnesses to the life of faith,
let us strip off every weight that slows us down,
especially the sin that so easily hinders our progress.
And let us run with endurance
the race that God has set before us.
We do this by keeping our eyes on Jesus,
on whom our faith depends from start to finish."

Hebrews 12:1–2 (NLT)

GLOSSARY

alembic—the top container of the glass distillation system that collects the vapors being distilled. The vapors travel into it through its long, narrow snout. When they cool, they go back their original liquid form but in a more purified state.

athanor—a tower-like furnace, fed by wood or charcoal. It is used to heat the solutions being distilled.

crucible—a small clay bowl that can be heated to high temperatures. It is often placed on a brick hearth above a hot fire of coals.

cucurbit—the bottom gourd-shaped container of the glass distillation system. It holds the original liquid being distilled.

distillation—a process where a liquid is boiled, its vapor travels to another container, and the vapor cools and returns back to a liquid state.

ferment—a yeast-like material that helps transform the substance it is added to.

"Great Work"—the lifetime process of trying to create the philosopher's stone.

lute—a sticky, glue-like mixture spread on a cloth that is used to seal the cucurbit and alembic together.

philsopher's stone—a substance that purportedly can turn base metals to gold and give immortality to anyone who drinks it. It is also called the red elixir.

Faith
Building
Guide

Ages
9 and up

Reverence

TREACHERY IN THE
ANCIENT LABORATORY

Spiritual Building Block: Reverence

THINK ABOUT IT

The Ten Commandments tell us a lot about God. They tell us what is important to him, what behaviors he loves and hates. They are like a recipe for holiness. If we do what they say, our lives will please God. We will be the kind of people he wants us to be, and our lives will show others what is important to him.

The third commandment talks about honoring God through his name. It says, "You shall not misuse the name of the LORD your God, for the LORD will not hold anyone guiltless who misuses his name" (Exodus 20:7).

After God spoke to the Israelites at Mount Sinai and gave them the Ten Commandments and the law, they responded by saying, "Everything the LORD has said we will do" (Exodus 24:3). By making this covenant or promise with God, they were agreeing that they were his special people. As a result, they became mirrors of God's glory. Every part of their lives showed the people around them what their God was all about.

We, too, honor God's name through our lives. Anyone can say they are a Christian, but the way they talk and live shows others what they think being a Christian is really about. In this book, two men, Pepik and Scottie, both claim to be alchemists who are seeking the same thing—the philosopher's stone—yet they live their lives in different ways. Pepik tries to honor God in everything he does. He prays constantly, works hard so he can bring glory to God, and takes good care of the people around him. Scottie sees life and alchemy completely differently. All he's interested in is the gold he thinks the stone can create, and he'll do anything to get it. He lies, cheats, and treats others badly. Even though Pepik and Scottie are opposite in almost every way, both men claim to be alchemists. Through their lives, each of them gives people around them different ideas about what alchemy is all about.

TALK ABOUT IT

Parents often name their children after a friend or relative. Sometimes they even choose a name simply because they like the way it sounds. This is different than the way names were chosen during Bible times. The Israelites believed that a name revealed the character of the person it belonged to—what that person was about—so names were chosen very carefully.

In the creation story, God named Adam, and Adam named Eve and the animals. Throughout the Bible, parents chose special names for their children, sometimes with God's help. Abraham and Sarah named their long awaited son Isaac, which means "he laughs," because Sarah was so happy to have a baby in her old age. An angel visited Zechariah, the father of John the Baptist, and told him what to name his son. Sometimes God changed people's names: Abram became Abraham after God made a special covenant with him, and Saul became Paul after he became a Christian.

There is one being whom no one could name—God. He gave himself a very special name in the Old Testament, "Yahweh." It means "I am who I am" in Hebrew, the original language of the Old Testament. This name that God gave himself was so precious that sometimes people didn't want to say it out loud, so they called God "Adonai," or "my

Lord" instead. Many bibles write the word "LORD" instead of "Yahweh."

The Bible has other names for God as well. Two examples are Jehovah Jireh, which means, "The Lord will provide," and El-Shaddai, or "God Almighty." The name "Jesus" came from the Hebrew word "Yeshua," which means "God the Savior," and the word "Christ" is Greek for "the anointed One." Jesus is also called "Immanuel," which means "God with us" in Hebrew. Each of these names reminded the people of a special way in which they had to come to know God and further understand his character.

When the third commandment says that we are to honor God's name, this is because his name is special—it tells us a lot about him—and we shouldn't take it lightly.

What does God's name mean to you? Is it something important you treat with respect? People often think the third commandment is just about swearing, but it includes a lot more than that. It goes together with the first two commandments, showing us how we are to think about God, and the place he should have in our lives. When people swear using God's name, they are revealing what they know and believe about God. If they truly know him as the creator and the God of the universe who possesses all power and wisdom and might, they wouldn't talk about him in this rude way. Their words show they don't know God, understand God, or love God.

The message of the third commandment is important for Christians. As God's covenant people, the way we live tells others what we believe about God. If we believe God is holy, as the Bible says he is, our lives should reflect the things that are important to him. We shouldn't purposely do anything that we know is not pleasing to God. If we say Jesus is our Lord, it should show in our lives through our thoughts, words, and deeds.

In Luke 6:46, Jesus says, "Why do you call me, 'Lord, Lord,' and do not do what I say?" The apostle John writes, "This is love for God: to obey his command" (1 John 5:3). Sometimes people go to church and sing songs and say prayers, but they don't love God in their hearts.

People who live like this are breaking the third commandment. If we say we believe in God, we must live in a way that honors him.

TRY IT

Jesus gave us the Lord's Prayer as a model for how we should talk to God. Read it out loud. If you don't know it by memory, you can find it in Matthew 6:9–13. Notice how the second part of the first sentence says, "hallowed be your name." Jesus understood that God's name was to be honored and only used in ways that would bring him glory.

If you think of your life as a mirror, do your thoughts, words, and actions reflect what you believe about God in your heart? If not, ask God to help you live in a way that is pleasing to him.

The Word at Work Around the World

A vital part of Cook Communications Ministries is our international outreach, Cook Communications Ministries International (CCMI). Your purchase of this book, and of other books and Christian-growth products from Cook, enables CCMI to provide Bibles and Christian literature to people in more than 150 languages in 65 countries.

Cook Communications Ministries is a not-for-profit, self-supporting organization. Revenues from sales of our books, Bible curricula, and other church and home products not only fund our U.S. ministry, but also fund our CCMI ministry around the world. One hundred percent of donations to CCMI go to our international literature programs.

CCMI reaches out internationally in three ways:

· Our premier International Christian Publishing Institute (ICPI) trains leaders from nationally led publishing houses around the world.

· We provide literature for pastors, evangelists, and Christian workers in their national language.

· We reach people at risk—refugees, AIDS victims, street children, and famine victims—with God's Word.

Word Power, God's Power

Faith Kidz, RiverOak, Honor, Life Journey, Victor, NexGen — every time you purchase a book produced by Cook Communications Ministries, you not only meet a vital personal need in your life or in the life of someone you love, but you're also a part of ministering to José in Colombia, Humberto in Chile, Gousa in India, or Lidiane in Brazil. You help make it possible for a pastor in China, a child in Peru, or a mother in West Africa to enjoy a life-changing book. And because you helped, children and adults around the world are learning God's Word and walking in his ways.

Thank you for your partnership in helping to disciple the world. May God bless you with the power of his Word in your life.

For more information about our international ministries, visit www.ccmi.org.